COSMIC ENGINEERS

The shell of the spaceship crawled with a dull, dead heat, the kind of heat that comes up off a dusty road on a still, hot day in August.

And soon, he knew, it would be a live heat, not a dead heat any longer, but a blasting furnace heat that would pour from every angle of the steel around them... But long before the leather of their shoes shriveled and curled, they would have to make their break, a hopeless dash for freedom that could end in nothing but death at the hands of the things that waited by the port...

**Also by Clifford D. Simak
in Magnum Books**

WAY STATION
CEMETERY WORLD
TIME IS THE SIMPLEST THING
SO BRIGHT THE VISION
SHAKESPEARE'S PLANET
ALL FLESH IS GRASS
A HERITAGE OF STARS
CATFACE

Cosmic Engineers

CLIFFORD D. SIMAK

MAGNUM BOOKS
Methuen Paperbacks Ltd.

A Magnum Book

COSMIC ENGINEERS
ISBN 0 417 05730 X

First published in United States 1964
by Paperback Library Inc
Magnum edition published 1982

Copyright © 1950 by Clifford D. Simak;
Copyright © 1978 renewed by Clifford D. Simak
From the original short novel by the same author,
Copyright © 1939 by Street and Smith Publications Inc.

Magnum Books are published by
Methuen Paperbacks Ltd
11 New Fetter Lane, London EC4P 4EE

Printed and bound in Great Britain by
Cox & Wyman Ltd, Reading

This book is sold subject to the condition that it shall not, by way of trade or otherwise, be lent, resold, hired out, or otherwise circulated without the publisher's prior consent in any form of binding or cover other than that in which it is published and without a similar condition including this condition being imposed on the subsequent purchaser.

to
My Father and Mother

". . . apart from your assignments, you must always be receptive to, be prepared for, and act upon all news potential from strange sources though it may lead you to the end of the solar system—perhaps even to the very edge of the universe . . ."

From the *Interplanetary Newsman's Manual*

Chapter One

HERB HARPER snapped on the radio and a voice snarled, billions of miles away: "Police ship 968. Keep watch for freighter *Vulcan* on the Earth-Venus run. Search ship for drugs. Believed to be . . ."

Herb spun the dial. A lazy voice floated through the ship: "Pleasure yacht *Helen,* three hours out of Sandebar. Have you any messages for us?"

He spun the dial again. The voice of Tim Donovan, radio's ace newscaster, rasped: "Tommy Evans will have to wait a few more days before attempting his flight to Alpha Centauri. The Solar Commerce commission claims to have found some faults in the construction of his new generators, but Tommy still insists that those generators will shoot him along at a speed well over that of light. Nevertheless, he has been ordered to bring his ship back to Mars so that technicians may check it before he finally takes off. Tommy is out on Pluto now, all poised for launching off into space beyond the solar system. At last reports he had made no move to obey the order of the commission. Tommy's backers, angered by the order, call it high-handed, charge there are politics back of it . . ."

Herb shut off the radio and walked to the door separating the living quarters of the *Space Pup* from the control room.

"Hear that, Gary?" he asked. "Maybe we'll get to see this guy, Evans, after all."

Gary Nelson, puffing at his foul, black pipe, scowled savagely at Herb. "Who wants to see that glory grabber?" he asked.

"What's biting you now?" asked Herb.

"Nothing," said Gary, "except Tommy Evans. Ever since we left Saturn we haven't heard a thing out of Donovan except this Tommy Evans."

Herb stared at his lanky partner.

"You sure got a bad case of space fever," he said. "You been like a dog with a sore head the last few days."

"Who wouldn't get space fever?" snapped Gary. He gestured out through the vision plate. "Nothing but space," he said. "Blackness with little stars. Stars that have forgotten how to twinkle. Going hundreds of miles a second and you wonder if you're moving. No change in scenery. A few square feet of space to live in. Black space pressing all about you, taunting you, trying to get in . . ."

He stopped and sat down limply in the pilot's chair.

"How about a game of chess?" asked Herb.

Gary twisted about and snapped at him:

"Don't mention chess to me again, you sawed-off shrimp. I'll space-walk you if you do. So help me Hannah if I won't."

"Thought maybe it would quiet you down," said Herb.

Gary leveled his pipestem at Herb.

"If I had the guy who invented three-way chess," he said, "I'd wring his blasted neck. The old kind was bad enough, but three-dimensional, twenty-seven man . . ."

He shook his head dismally.

"He must have been half nuts," he said.

"He did go off his rockers," Herb told him, "but not from inventing three-way chess. Guy by the name of Konrad Fairbanks. In an asylum back on Earth now. I took a picture of him once, when he was coming out of the courtroom. Just after the judge said he was only half there. The cops chased hell out of me but I got away. The Old Man paid me ten bucks bonus for the shot."

"I remember that," said Gary. "Best mathematical mind in the whole system. Worked out equations no one could understand. Went screwy when he proved that there actually were times when one and one didn't quite make two. Proved it, you understand. Not just theory or mathematical mumbo-jumbo."

Herb walked across the control room and stood beside Gary, looking out through the vision plate.

"Everything been going all right?" he asked.

Gary growled deep in his throat.

"What could go wrong out here? Not even any meteors. Nothing to do but sit and watch. And there really isn't any need of that. The robot navigator handles everything."

The soft purr of the geosectors filled the ship. There was no other sound. The ship seemed standing still in space. Saturn swung far down to the right, a golden disk of light with thin, bright rings. Pluto was a tiny speck of light almost dead ahead, a little to the left. The Sun, three billion miles astern, was shielded from their sight.

The *Space Pup* was headed for Pluto at a pace that neared a thousand miles a second. The geosectors, warping the curvature of space itself, hurled the tiny ship through the void at a speed unthought of less than a hundred years before.

And now Tommy Evans, out on Pluto, was ready, if only the Solar Commerce commission would stop its interference, to bullet his experimental craft away from the solar system, out toward the nearest star, 4.29 light-years distant. Providing his improved electro-gravatic geodesic deflectors lived up to the boast of their inventors, he would exceed the speed of light, would vanish into that limbo of impossibility that learned savants only a few centuries before had declared was unattainable.

"It kind of makes a fellow dizzy," Herb declared.

"What does?"

"Why," said Herb, "this Tommy Evans stunt. The boy is making history. And maybe we'll be there to see him do it. He's the first to make a try at the stars—and if he wins, there will be lots of others. Man will go out and out . . . and still farther out, maybe clear out to where space is still exploding."

Gary grunted. "They sure will have to hurry some," he said, "because space is exploding fast."

"Now look here," said Herb. "You can't just sit there and pretend the human race has made no progress. Take this ship, just for example. We don't rely on rockets any more except in taking off and landing. Once out in space and we set the geosectors to going and we warp space and build up speed that no rocket could ever hope to give you. We got an atmosphere generator that manufactures air. No more stocking up on oxygen and depending on air purifiers. Same thing with food. The machine just picks up matter and energy out of space and transmutes them into steaks and potatoes—or at least their equivalent in food value. And we send news stories and pictures across billions of miles of space. You just sit down in front of that spacewriter and whang away at the keys and in a few hours another machine back in New York writes what you have written."

Gary yawned. "How you run on," he said. "We haven't even started yet—the human race hasn't. What we have done isn't anything to what we are going to do. That is, if the race doesn't get so downright ornery that it kills itself off first."

The spacewriter in the corner of the room stuttered and gibbered, warming up under the impulse of the warning signals, flung out hours before and three billion miles away.

The two men hurried across the room and hung over it. Slowly, laboriously, the keys began to tap.

NELSON, ABOARD SPACE PUP, NEARING PLUTO. HAVE INFO EVANS MAY TAKE OFF FOR CENTAURI WITHOUT AUTHORIZATION OF SCC. MAKE ALL POSSIBLE SPEED TO PLUTO. HANDLE SOONEST. MOST IMPORTANT. RUSH. REGARDS. EVENING ROCKET.

The machine burped to a stop. Herb looked at Gary.

"Maybe that guy Evans has got some guts after all," said Gary. "Maybe he'll tell the SCC where to stick it. They been asking for it for a long time now."

Herb grunted. "They won't chase after him, that's sure."

Gary sat down before the sending board and threw the switch. The hum of the electric generators drowned out the moan of the geosectors as they built up the power necessary to hurl a beam of energy across the void to Earth.

"Only one thing wrong with this setup," said Gary. "It takes too long and it takes too much power. I wish someone would hurry up and figure out a way to use the cosmics for carriers."

"Doc Kingsley, out on Pluto, has been fooling around with cosmics," said Herb. "Maybe he'll turn the trick in another year of two."

"Doc Kingsley has been fooling around with a lot of

things out there," said Gary. "If the man would only talk, we'd have more than one story to send back from Pluto."

The dynamos had settled into a steady hum of power. Gary glanced at the dials and reached out his fingers. He wrote:

> EVENING ROCKET. EARTH. WILL CONTACT EVANS AT ONCE IF STILL ON PLUTO. IF NOT WILL SEND STORY ON FLIGHT. NOTHING TO REPORT OUT HERE. WEATHER FINE. HERB DROPPED OUR LAST QUART AND BROKE IT. HOW ABOUT A RAISE.

"That last," he said, "will get 'em."

"You didn't have to put that in about the Scotch," Herb declared. "It just slipped out of my fingers."

"Sure," said Gary. "It just slipped out of your fingers. Right smack-dab onto a steel plate and busted all to hell. After this, I handle the liquor. When you want a drink, you ask me."

"Maybe Kingsley will have some liquor," Herb said hopefully. "Maybe he'll lend us a bottle."

"If he does," declared Gary, "you keep your paws off of it. Between you sucking away at it and dropping it, I don't get more than a drink or two out of each bottle. We still got Uranus and Neptune to do after Pluto and it looks like a long dry spell."

He got up and walked to the fore part of the ship, gazing out through the vision plate.

"Only Neptune and Uranus ahead," he said. "And that's enough. If the Old Man ever thinks up any more screwball stunts, he can find someone else to do them. When I get back I'm going to ask him to give me back my old beat at the space terminal and I'm going to settle down there for the rest of my natural life. I'm going to watch the ships come in and take off and I'm going to get down on my hands and knees and kiss the ground each time and be thankful I'm not on them."

"He's paying us good dough," said Herb. "We got bank accounts piling up back home."

Gary pretended not to hear him.

"Know Your Solar System," he said. "Special articles run every Sunday in the *Evening Rocket*. Story by Gary Nelson. Pictures by Herbert Harper. Intrepid newsmen brave perils of space to bring back true picture of the solar system's planets. One year alone in a spaceship, bringing to the readers of the *Rocket* a detailed account of life in space, of life on the planets. Remember how the promotion gang busted a gut advertising us. Full page ads and everything."

He spat.

"Stuff for kids," he said.

"The kids probably think we're heroes," said Herb. "Probably they read our stuff and then pester the folks to buy them a spaceship. Want to go out and see Saturn for themselves."

"The Old Man said it would boost circulation," declared Gary. "Hell, he'd commit suicide if he thought it would boost circulation. Remember what he told us. Says he: 'Go out and visit all the planets. Get first-hand information and pictures. Shoot them back to us. We'll run them every Sunday in the magazine section.' Just like he was sending us around the corner to cover a fire. That's all there was to it. Just a little over a year out in space. Living in a spaceship and a spacesuit. Hurry through Jupiter's moons to get out to Saturn and then take it on the lam for Pluto. Soft job. Nice vacation for you. That's what the Old Man said. Nice soft vacation, he said."

His pipe gurgled threateningly and he knocked it out viciously against the heel of his hand.

"Well," said Herb, "we're almost to Pluto. A few days more and we'll be there. They got a fueling station and a radio and Doc Kingsley's laboratories out there. Maybe we can promote us a poker game."

Gary walked to the telescopic screen and switched it on.

"Let's take a look at her," he said.

The great circular screen glowed softly. Within it swam the image of Pluto, still almost half a billion miles away. A dead planet that shone dully in the faint light of the far distant Sun. A planet locked in the frigid grip of naked space, a planet that had been dead long before the first stirring of life had taken place on Earth.

The vision was blurred and Gary manipulated dials to bring it more sharply into focus.

"Wait a second," snapped Herb. His fingers reached out and grasped Gary's wrist.

"Turn it back a ways," he said. "I saw something out there. Something that looked like a ship. Maybe it's Evans coming back."

Slowly Gary twisted the dial back. A tiny spot of light danced indistinctly on the screen.

"That's it," breathed Herb. "Easy now. Just a little more."

The spot of light leaped into sharper focus. But it was merely a spot of light, nothing more, a tiny, shining thing in space. Some metallic body that was catching and reflecting the light of the Sun.

"Give it more power," said Herb.

Swiftly the spot of light grew, assumed definite shape. Gary stepped the magnification up until the thing filled the entire screen.

It was a ship—and yet it couldn't be a ship.

"It has no rocket tubes," said Herb in amazement. "Without tubes how could it get off the ground? You can't use geosectors in taking off. They twist space all to hell and gone. They'd turn a planet inside out."

Gary studied it. "It doesn't seem to be moving," he said. "Maybe some motion, but not enough to detect."

"A derelict," suggested Herb.

Gary shook his head. "Still doesn't explain the lack of tubes," he said.

The two men lifted their eyes from the screen and looked at one another.

"The Old Man said we were to hurry to Pluto," Herb reminded Gary.

Gary wheeled about and strode back to the controls. He lowered his gangling frame into the pilot's chair and disconnected the robot control. His fingers reached out, switched off the geosectors, pumped fuel into the rocket chambers.

"Find something to hang onto," he said, grimly. "We're stopping to see what this is all about."

Chapter Two

THE mysterious space-shell was only a few miles distant. With Herb at the controls, the *Space Pup* cruised in an ever-tightening circle around the glinting thing that hung there just off Pluto's orbit.

It was a spaceship. Of that there could be no doubt despite the fact that it had no rocket tubes. It was hanging motionless. There was no throb of power within it, no apparent life, although dim light glowed through the vision ports in what probably were the living quarters just back of the control room.

Gary crouched in the airlock of the *Space Pup,* with the outer valve swung back. He made sure that his pistols were securely in their holsters and cautiously tested the spacesuit's miniature propulsion units.

He spoke into his helmet mike.

"All right, Herb," he said, "I'm going. Try to tighten up the circle a bit. Keep a close watch. That thing out there may be dynamite."

"Keep your nose clean," said Herb's voice in the phones.

Gary straightened and pushed himself out from the lock. He floated smoothly in space, in a gulf of nothing, a place without direction, without an up or down, an unsubstantial place with the fiery eyes of distant stars ringing him around.

His steel-gloved hand dropped to the propulsion mechanism that encircled his waist. Midget rocket tubes flared with tiny flashes of blue power and he was jerked forward, heading for the mystery ship. Veering too far to the right, he gave the right tube a little more fuel and straightened out.

Steadily, under the surging power of the spacesuit tubes, he forged ahead through space toward the ship. He saw the gleaming lights of the *Space Pup* slowly circle in front of him and then pass out of sight.

A quarter of a mile away, he shut off the tubes and

glided slowly in to the drifting shell. He struck its pitted side with the soles of his magnetic boots and stood upright.

Cautiously he worked his way toward one of the ports from which came the faint gleam of light. Lying at full length, he peered through the foot-thick quartz. The light was feeble and he could see but little. There was no movement of life, no indication that the shell was tenanted. In the center of what at one time had been the living quarters, he saw a large rectangular shape, like a huge box. Aside from this, however, he could make out nothing.

Working his way back to the lock, he saw that it was tightly closed. He had expected that. He stamped against the plates with his heavy boots, hoping to attract attention. But if any living thing were inside, it either did not hear or disregarded the clangor that he made.

Slowly he moved away from the lock, heading for the control-room vision plate, hoping from there to get a better view into the shell's interior. As he moved, his eyes caught a curious irregularity just to the right of the lock, as if faint lines had been etched into the steel of the hull.

He dropped to one knee and saw that a single line of crude lettering had been etched into the metal. Brushing at it with his gloved hand, he tried to make it out. Laboriously, he struggled with it. It was simple, direct, to the point, a single declaration. When one writes with steel and acid, one is necessarily brief.

The line read:

Control room vision-plate unlocked.

Amazed, he read the line again, hardly believing what he read. But there it was. That single line, written with a single purpose. Simple directions for gaining entrance.

Crouched upon the steel plating, he felt a shiver run through his body. Someone had etched that line in hope that someone would come. But perhaps he was too late. The ship had an old look about it. The lines of it, the way the ports were set into the hull, all were marks of spaceship designing that had become obsolete centuries before.

He felt the cold chill of mystery and the utter bleakness of outer space closing in about him. He gazed up over the bulged outline of the shell and saw the steely glare of remote stars. Stars secure in the depth of many light-years, jeering at him, jeering at men who held dreams of stellar conquest.

He shook himself, trying to shake off the probing fingers of half-fear, glanced around to locate the *Space Pup,* saw it slowly moving off to his right.

Swiftly, but carefully, he made his way over the nose of the ship and up to the vision plate.

Squatting in front of the plate, he peered down into the control cabin. But it wasn't a control cabin. It was a laboratory. In the tiny room which at one time must have housed the instruments of navigation, there was now no trace of control panel or calculator or telescopic screen. Rather, there were work tables, piled with scientific apparatus, banks and rows of chemical containers. All the paraphernalia of the scientist's workshop.

The door into the living quarters, where he had seen the large oblong box was closed. All the apparatus and the bottles in the laboratory were carefully arranged, neatly put away, as if someone had tidied up before they walked off and left the place.

He puzzled for a moment. That lack of rocket tubes, the indications that the ship was centuries old, the scrawled acid-etched line by the lock, the laboratory in the control room . . . what did it all add up to? He shook his head. It didn't make much sense.

Bracing himself against the curving steel hide of the shell, he pushed at the vision-plate. But he could exert little effort. Lack of gravity, inability to brace himself securely, made the task a hard one. Rising to his feet, he stamped his heavy boots against the glass, but the plate refused to budge.

As a last desperate effort, he might use his guns, blast his way into the shell. But that would be long, tedious work . . . and there would be a certain danger. There should be, he told himself, an easier and a safer way.

Suddenly the way came to him, but he hesitated, for there lay danger, too. He could lie down on the plate, turn on the rocket tubes of his suit and use his body as a battering ram, as a lever, to force the stubborn hinges.

But it would be an easy matter to turn on too much power, so much power that his body would be pounded to a pulp against the heavy quartz.

Shrugging at the thought, he stretched flat on the plate, hands folded under him with fingers on the tube controls. Slowly he turned the buttons. The rockets thrust at his body, jamming him against the quartz. He snapped the studs shut. It had seemed, for a moment, that the plate had given just a little.

Drawing in a deep breath, he twisted the studs again. Once more his body slammed against the plate, driven by the flaming tubes.

Suddenly the plate gave way, swung in and plunged him down into the laboratory. Savagely he snapped the studs shut. He struck hard against the floor, cracked his helmet soundly.

Groggily he groped his way to his feet. The thin whine of escaping atmosphere came to his ears and unsteadily he made his way forward. Leaping at the plate, he slammed it back into place again. It closed with a thud, driven deep into its frame by the force of rushing air.

A chair stood beside a table and he swung around, sat down in it, still dizzy from the fall. He shook his head to clear away the cobwebs.

There was atmosphere here. That meant that an atmosphere generator still was operating, that the ship had developed no leaks and was still airtight.

He raised his helmet slightly. Fresh pure air swirled into his nostrils, better air than he had inside his suit. A little highly oxygenated, perhaps, but that was all. If the atmosphere machine had run for a long time unattended, it might have gotten out of adjustment slightly, might be mixing a bit too much oxygen with the air output.

He swung the helmet back and let it dangle on the hinge at the back of the neck, gulped in great mouthfuls of the atmosphere. His head cleared rapidly.

He looked around the room. There was little that he had not already seen. A practical, well-equipped laboratory, but much of the equipment, he now realized, was old. Some of it was obsolete and that fitted in with all the rest of it.

A framed document hung above a cabinet and getting to his feet, he walked across the room to look at it. Bending close, he read it. It was a diploma from the College of Science at Alkatoon, Mars, one of the most outstanding of several universities on the Red Planet. The diploma had been issued to one Caroline Martin.

Gary read the name a second time. It seemed that he should know it. It raised some memory in his brain, but just what it was he couldn't say, an elusive recognition that eluded him by the faintest margin.

He looked around the room.

Caroline Martin.

A girl who had left a diploma in this cabin, a pitiful reminder of many years ago. He bent again and looked at the date upon the sheep-skin. It was 5976. He whistled softly. A thousand years ago!

A thousand years. And if Caroline Martin had left this diploma here a thousand years ago, where was Caroline Martin now? What had happened to her? Dead in what strange corner of the solar system? Dead in this very ship?

He swung about and strode toward the door that led into the living quarters. His hand reached out and seized the door and pushed it open. He took one step across the threshold and then he stopped, halted in his stride.

In the center of the room was the oblong box that he had seen from the port. But instead of a box, it was a tank, bolted securely to the floor by heavy steel brackets.

The tank was filled with a greenish fluid and in the fluid lay a woman, a woman dressed in metallic robes that sparkled in the light from the single radium bulb in the ceiling just above the tank.

Breathlessly, Gary moved closer, peered over the edge of the tank, down through the clear green liquid into the face of the woman. Her eyes were closed and long, curling black lashes lay against the whiteness of her cheeks. Her forehead was high and long braids of raven hair were bound about her head. Slim black eyebrows arched to almost meet above the delicately modeled nose. Her mouth was a thought too large, a trace of the patrician in the thin, red lips. Her arms were laid straight along her sides and the metallic gown swept in flowing curves from chin to ankles.

Beside her right hand, lying in the bottom of the tank, was a hypodermic syringe, bright and shining despite the green fluid which covered it.

Gary's breath caught in his throat.

She looked alive and yet she couldn't be alive. Still there was a flush of youth and beauty in her cheeks, as if she merely slept.

Laid out as if for death and still with the lie to death in her very look. Her face was calm, serene . . . and something else. Expectancy, perhaps. As if she only waited for a thing she hoped to happen.

Caroline Martin was the name on the diploma out in the laboratory. Could this be Caroline Martin? Could this be the girl who had graduated from the college of science at Alkatoon ten centuries ago?

Gary shook his head uneasily.

He stepped back from the tank and as he did he saw the copper plate affixed to its metal side. He stooped to read.

Another simple message, etched in copper . . . a message from the girl who lay inside the tank.

I am not dead. I am in suspended animation. Drain the tank by opening the valve. Use the syringe you find in the medicine cabinet.

Gary glanced across the room, saw a medicine chest on the wall above a washbowl. He looked back at the tank and mopped his brow with his coat sleeve.

"It isn't possible," he whispered.

Like a man in a dream, he stumbled to the medicine chest. The syringe was there. He broke it and saw that it was loaded with a cartridge filled with a reddish substance. A drug, undoubtedly, to overcome suspended animation.

Replacing the syringe, he went back to the tank and found the valve. It was stubborn with the years, defying all the strength in his arms. He kicked it with a heavy boot and jarred it loose. With nervous hands he opened it and watched the level of the green fluid slowly recede.

Watching, an odd calm came upon him, a steadying calm that made him hard and machine-like to do the thing that faced him. One little slip might spoil it. One fumbling move might undo the work of a thousand years. What if the drug in the hypodermic had lost its strength? There were so many things that might happen.

But there was only one thing to do. He raised a hand in front of him and looked at it. It was a steady hand.

He wasted no time in wondering what it was about. This was not the time for that. Frantic questionings clutched at his thoughts and he shook them off. Time enough to wonder and to speculate and question when this thing was done.

When the fluid was level with the girl's body, he waited no longer. He leaned over the rim of the tank and lifted her in his arms. For a moment he hesitated, then turned and went to the laboratory and placed her on one of the work tables. The fluid, dripping off the rustling metallic dress, left a trail of wet across the floor.

From the medicine chest he took the hypodermic and went back to the girl. He lifted her left arm and peered closely at it. There were little punctures, betraying previous use of the needle.

Perspiration stood out on his forehead. If only he knew a little more about this. If only he had some idea of what he was supposed to do.

Awkwardly he shoved the needle into a vein, depressed the plunger. It was done and he stepped back.

Nothing happened. He waited.

Minutes passed and she took a shallow breath. He watched in fascination, saw her come to life again . . . saw the breath deepen, the eyelids flicker, the right hand twitch.

Then she was looking at him out of deep blue eyes.

"You are all right?" he asked.

It was, he knew, a rather foolish question.

Her speech was broken. Her tongue and lips refused to work the way they should, but he understood what she tried to say.

"Yes, I'm all right." She lay quietly on the table. "What year is this?" she asked.

"It's 6948," he told her.

Her eyes widened and she looked at him with a startled

glance. "Almost a thousand years," she said. "You are sure of the year?"

He nodded. "That is about the only thing that I am really sure of."

"How is that?"

"Why, finding you here," said Gary, "and reviving you again. I still don't believe it happened."

She laughed, a funny, discordant laugh because her muscles, inactive for years, had forgotten how to function rightly.

"You are Caroline Martin, aren't you?" asked Gary.

She gave him a quick look of surprise and rose to a sitting position.

"I am Caroline Martin," she answered. "But how did you know that?"

Gary gestured at the diploma. "I read it."

"Oh," she said. "I'd forgotten all about it."

"I am Gary Nelson," he told her. "Newsman on the loose. My pal's out there in a spaceship waiting for us."

"I suppose," she said, "that I should thank you, but I don't know how. Just ordinary thanks aren't quite enough."

"Skip it," said Gary, tersely.

She stretched her arms above her head.

"It's good to be alive again," she said. "Good to know there's life ahead of you."

"But," said Gary, "you always were alive. It must have been just like going to sleep."

"It wasn't sleep," she said. "It was worse than death. Because, you see, I made one mistake."

"One mistake?"

"Yes, just one mistake. One you'd never think of. At least, I didn't. You see, when animation was suspended every physical process was reduced to almost zero, metabolism slowed down to almost nothing. But with one exception. My brain kept right on working."

The horror of it sank into Gary slowly. "You mean you knew?"

She nodded. "I couldn't hear or see or feel. I had no bodily sensation. But I could think. I've thought for almost ten centuries. I tried to stop thinking, but I never could.

I prayed something would go wrong and I would die. Anything at all to end that eternity of thought."

She saw the pity in his eyes.

"Don't waste sympathy on me," she said and there was a note of hardness in her voice. "I brought it on myself. Stubbornness, perhaps. I played a long shot. I took a gamble."

He chuckled in his throat. "And won."

"A billion to one shot," she said. "Probably greater odds than that. It was madness itself to do it. This shell is a tiny speck in space. There wasn't, I don't suppose, a billion-to-one chance, if you figured it out on paper, that anyone would find me. I had some hope. Hope that would have reduced those odds somewhat. I placed my faith on someone and I guess they failed me. Perhaps it wasn't their fault. Maybe they died before they could even hunt for me."

"But how did you do it?" asked Gary. "Even today suspended animation has our scientists stumped. They've made some progress but not much. And you made it work a thousand years ago."

"Drugs," she said. "Certain Martian drugs. Rare ones. And they have to be combined correctly. Slow metabolism to a point where it is almost non-existent. But you have to be careful. Slow it down too far and metabolism stops. That's death."

Gary gestured toward the hypodermic. "And that," he said, "reacts against the other drug."

She nodded gravely.

"The fluid in the tank," he said. "That was to prevent dehydration and held some food value? You wouldn't need much food with metabolism at nearly zero. But how about your mouth and nostrils? The fluid . . ."

"A mask," she said. "Chemical paste that held up under moisture. Evaporated as soon as it was struck by air."

"You thought of everything."

"I had to," she declared. "There was no one else to do my thinking for me."

She slid off the table and walked slowly toward him. "You told me a minute ago," she said, "that the scientists of today haven't satisfactorily solved suspended animation."

He nodded.

"You mean to say they still don't know about these drugs?"

"There are some of them," he said, "who'd give their good right arm to know about them."

"We knew about them a thousand years ago," the girl said. "Myself and one other. I wonder . . ."

She whirled on Gary. "Let's get out of here," she cried. "I have a horror of this place."

"Anything you want to take?" he asked. "Anything I can get together for you?"

She made an impatient gesture.

"No," she said. "I want to forget this place."

Chapter Three

THE *Space Pup* arrowed steadily toward Pluto. From the engine room came the subdued hum of the geosectors. The vision plate looked out on ebon space with its far-flung way posts of tiny, steely stars. The needle was climbing up near the thousand-miles-a-second mark.

Caroline Martin leaned forward in her chair and stared out at the vastness that stretched eternally ahead. "I could stay and watch forever," she exulted.

Gary, lounging back in the pilot's seat, said quietly: "I've been thinking about that name of yours. It seems to me I've heard it somewhere. Read it in a book."

She glanced at him swiftly and then stared out into space.

"Perhaps you have," she said finally.

There was a silence, unbroken except by the humming of the geosectors.

The girl turned back to Gary, chin cupped in her hands.

"Probably you have read about me," she said. "Perhaps the name of Caroline Martin is mentioned in your histories.

You see, I was a member of the old Mars-Earth Research commission during the war with Jupiter. I was so proud of the appointment. Just four years out of school and I was trying so hard to get a good job in some scientific research work. I wanted to earn money to go back to school again."

"I'm beginning to remember now," said Gary, "but there must be something wrong. The histories say you were a traitor. They say you were condemned to death."

"I was a traitor," she said and there was a thread of ancient bitterness in the words she spoke. "I refused to turn over a discovery I made, a discovery that would have won the war. It also would have wrecked the solar system. I told them so, but they were men at war. They were desperate men. We were losing then."

"We never did win, really," Gary told her.

"They condemned me to space," she said. "They put me in that shell you found me in and a war cruiser towed it out to Pluto's orbit and cut it loose. It was an old condemned craft, its machinery outmoded. They ripped out the rockets and turned it into a prison for me."

She made a gesture of silence at the shocked look on their faces.

"The histories don't tell that part of it," said Herb.

"They probably suppressed it," she said. "Men at war will do things that no sane man will do. They would not admit in peace the atrocities that they committed in the time of battle. They put the laboratory in the control room as a final ironic jest. So I could carry out my research, they said. Research, they told me, I'd not need to turn over to them."

"Would your discovery have wrecked the system?" Gary asked.

"Yes," she said, "it would have. That's why I refused to give it to the military board. For that they called me traitor. I think they hoped to break me. I think they thought up to the very last that, faced with exile in space, I would finally crack and give it to them."

"When you didn't," Herb said, "they couldn't back down. They couldn't afford to let you call their bluff."

"They never found your notes," said Gary.

She tapped her forehead with a slender finger. "My notes were here," she said.

He looked amazed.

"And still are," she said.

"But how did you get the drugs to carry out your suspended animation?" Gary asked.

She waited for long minutes.

"That's the part I hate to think about," she said. "The part that's hard to think about. I worked with a young man. About my age, then. He must be dead these many years."

She stopped and Gary could see that she was trying to marshal in her mind what next to say.

"We were in love," she said. "Together we discovered the suspended animation process. We had worked on it secretly for months and were ready to announce it when I was taken before the military tribunal. They never let me see him after that. I was allowed no visitors.

"Out in space, after the war cruiser left, I almost went insane. I invented all sorts of tasks to do. I arranged and rearranged my chemicals and apparatus and then one day I found the drugs, skillfully hidden in a box of chemicals. Only one person in the world besides myself knew about them. I found the drugs and two hypodermic syringes."

Gary's pipe had gone out and now he relit it.

The girl went on.

"I knew it would be a gamble," she said. "I knew he intended that I should take that gamble. Maybe he had a wild scheme of coming out and hunting for me. Maybe something happened and he couldn't come. Maybe he tried and failed. Maybe the war . . . got him. But he had given me a chance, a desperate chance to beat the fate the military court had set for me. I removed the steel partition in the engine room to make the tank. That took many weeks. I etched the copper plate. I went outside on the shell and etched the lines beside the lock. I'm afraid that wasn't a very good job."

"And then," said Herb, "you put yourself to sleep."

"Not exactly sleep," she said. "Because my brain still worked. I thought and thought for almost a thousand years. My mind set up problems and worked them out. I developed a flair for pure deduction, since my mind was the only thing left for me to work with. I believe I even developed telepathic powers."

"You mean," asked Herb, "that you can read our thoughts?"

She nodded, then hastened on. "But I wouldn't," she said. "I wouldn't do that to my friends. I knew when Gary first came to the shell. I read the wonder and amazement in his thoughts. I was so afraid he'd go away and leave me alone again. I tried to talk to him with my thoughts, but he was so upset that he couldn't understand."

Gary shook his head. "Anyone would have been upset," he said.

"But," exploded Herb, "think of the chances that you took. It was just pure luck we found you. Your drug wouldn't have held up forever. Another few thousand years, perhaps, but scarcely longer than that. Then there would be the chance that the atmosphere generators might have failed. Or that a big meteor, or even a small one, for that matter, might have come along. There were a thousand things that could have happened."

She agreed with him. "It was a long chance. I knew it was. But there was no other way. I could have just sat still and done nothing or gone crazy, grown old and died in loneliness."

She was silent for a moment.

"It would have been easy," she said then, "if I hadn't made that one mistake."

"Weren't you frightened?" Gary asked.

Her eyes widened slightly and she nodded.

"I heard voices," she said. "Voices coming out of space, out of the void that lies between the galaxies. Things talking over many light-years with one another. Things to which the human race, intellectually, would appear mere insects. At first I was frightened, frightened at the things they said, at the horrible hints I sensed in the things I couldn't understand. Then, growing desperate, I tried to talk back to them, tried to attract their attention. I wasn't afraid of them any more and I thought that they might help. I didn't care much what happened any more just so someone, or something, would help me. Even take notice of me. Anything to let me know that I wasn't all alone."

Gary lit his pipe again and silence fell for just a space.

"Voices," said Herb.

They all stared out at that darkness that hemmed them in. Gary felt the hairs bristle at the nape of his neck. Some cold wind from far away had brushed against his face, an unnamable terror out of the cosmos reaching out for him, searching for him with dirty-taloned thoughts. Things that hurled pure thought across the deserts of emptiness that lay between the galaxies.

"Tell me," said Caroline, and her voice, too, seemed to come from far away, "how did the war come out?"

"The war?" asked Gary.

Then he understood.

"Oh, the war," he said. "Why, Earth and Mars finally won out. Or so the histories claim. There was a battle out near Ganymede and both fleets limped home badly beaten up. The Jovians went back to Jupiter, the Earth-Mars fleet pulled into Sandebar on Mars. For months the two inner planets built up their fleets and strengthened home defenses. But the Jovians never came out again and our fleets didn't dare carry the war to the enemy. Even today we haven't developed a ship that dares go into Jupiter's atmosphere. Our geosectors might take us there and bring us back, but you can't use them near a planetary body. They work on the principle of warping space..."

"Warping space?" asked the girl, suddenly sitting upright.

"Sure," said Gary. "Anything peculiar about it?"

"No," she said, "I don't suppose there is."

Then: "I wouldn't exactly call that a victory."

"That's what the histories call it." Gary shrugged. "They claim we run the Jovians to cover and they've been afraid to come out ever since. Earth and Mars have taken over Jupiter's moons and colonized them, but to this day no one has sighted a Jovian or a Jovian ship. Not since that day back in 5980.

"It's just one of them things," Herb decided for them.

The girl was staring out at space again. Hungry for see-

ing, hungry for living, but with the scars of awful memories etched into her brain.

Gary shivered to himself. Alone, she had taken her gamble and had won. Won against time and space and the brutality of man and the great indifference of the mighty sweep of stars.

What had she thought of during those long years? What problems had she solved? What kind of a person could she be, with her twenty-year-old body and her thousand-year-old brain?

Gary nursed the hot bowl of his pipe between his hands, studying the outline of her head against the vision-plate. Square chin, high forehead, the braided strands wrapped around her head.

What was she thinking now? Of that lover who now would be forgotten dust? Of how he might have tried to find her, of how he might have searched through space and failed? Or was she thinking of the voices . . . the voices talking back and forth across the gulfs of empty space?

The spacewriter, sitting in its own dark corner, broke into a gibbering chatter.

Gary sprang to his feet.

"Now what?" he almost shouted.

The chattering ceased and the machine settled into the click-clack of its message.

Gary hurried forward. The other two pressed close behind, looking over his shoulder.

NELSON, ABOARD SPACE PUP, NEARING PLUTO. KINGSLEY REPORTS RECEIVING STRANGE MESSAGES FROM SOMEWHERE OUT OF THE SOLAR SYSTEM. UNABLE, OR UNWILLING, TO GUESS AT SOURCE. REFUSES TO GIVE CIRCUMSTANCES UNDER WHICH MESSAGES WERE RECEIVED OR CONTEXT OF THEM, IF IN FACT HE KNOWS CONTEXT. URGENT THAT YOU GET STATEMENT FROM HIM SOONEST. REGARDS. EVENING ROCKET.

The machine's stuttering came to an end.

The three stared at one another.

"Messages," said Herb. "Messages out of space."

Gary shook his head. He stole a swift glance at the girl and her face seemed pale. Perhaps she was remembering.

Chapter Four

TRAIL'S END, Pluto's single community, cowering at the foot of a towering black mountain, seemed deserted. There was no stir of life about the buildings that huddled between the spacefield and the mountain. The spiraling tower of the radio station climbed dizzily spaceward and beside it squatted the tiny radio shack. Behind it stood the fueling station and the hangar, while half a mile away loomed the larger building that housed the laboratories of the Solar Science commission.

Caroline moved closer to Gary.

"It seems so lonely," she whispered. "I don't like loneliness now . . . after . . ."

Gary stirred uneasily, scraping the heavy boots of his spacesuit over the pitted rock. "It's always lonely enough," he said. "I wonder where they are."

As he spoke the lock of the radio shack opened and a space-suited figure strode across the field to meet them.

His voice crackled in their helmet phones. "You must be Nelson," it said. "I'm Ted Smith, operator here. Kingsley told me to bring you up to the house right away."

"Fine," said Gary. "Glad to be here. I suppose Evans is still around."

"He is," said Smith. "He's up at the house now. His ship is in the hangar. Personally, I figure he's planning to take off and let the SCC do what they can about it."

Smith fell in step with them. "It's good to see new faces," he declared, "especially a woman. We don't have women visitors very often."

"I'm sorry," said Gary. "I forgot."

He introduced Caroline and Herb to Smith as they

plodded past the radio shack and started for the laboratory.

"It gets God-lonesome out here," said Smith. "This is a hellish place, if I do say so myself. No wind. No moon. No nothing. Very little difference between day and night because there's never any clouds to cover the stars and even in the daytime the Sun is little better than a star."

His tongue, loosened by visitors to talk to, rambled on.

"A fellow gets kind of queer out here," he told them. "It's enough to make anyone get queer. I think the doctor is half crazy from staying here too long. He thinks he's getting messages from some place far away. Acts mysterious about it."

"You think he just imagines it?" asked Herb.

"I'm not saying one way or the other," declared Smith, "but I ask you ... where would you get the messages from? Think of the power it would take just to send a message from Alpha Centauri. And that isn't so very far away. Not so far as stars go. Right next door, you might say."

"Evans is going to fly there and back," Herb reminded him.

"Evans is space-nuts," said Smith. "With all the solar system to fool around in, he has to go gallivanting off to the stars. He hasn't got a chance. I told him so, but he laughed at me. I'm sorry for him. He's a nice young fellow."

They mounted the steps, hewn out of living stone, which led to the main airlock of the laboratory building. Smith pressed a button and they waited.

"I suppose you'll want Andy to go over your ship," Smith suggested.

"Sure," said Gary. "Tell him to take good care of it."

"Andy is the fueling-station man," the radio operator explained. "But he hasn't much to do now. Most of the ships use geosectors. There's only a few old tubs, one or two a year, that need any fuel. Used to be a good business, but not any more."

The space lock swung open and the three stepped inside. Smith remained by the doorway.

"I have to go back to the shack," he said. "I'll see you again before you leave."

The lock hissed shut behind them and the inner screw began to turn. It swung open and they stepped into a small room that was lined with spacesuits hanging on the wall.

A man was standing in the center of the room. A big man, with broad shoulders and hands like hams. His unruly shock of hair was jet-black and his voice boomed jovially at them.

"Glad to see all of you," he said and laughed, a deep, thunderous laugh that seemed to shake the room.

Gary swung back the helmet of his suit and thrust out a gloved hand.

"You are Dr. Kingsley?" he asked.

"That's who I am," boomed the mighty voice. "And who are these folks with you?"

Gary introduced them.

"I didn't know there was a lady in the party," said the doctor.

"There wasn't," said Herb. "Not until just recently."

"Mean to tell me they've taken to hitch-hiking out in space?"

Gary laughed. "Even better than that, doctor," he said. "There's a little story about Miss Martin you'll enjoy."

"Come on," he roared at them. "Get out of your duds. I got some coffee brewing. And you'll want to meet Tommy Evans. He's that young fool who thinks he's going to fly four light-years out to old A.C."

And at just that moment Tommy Evans burst into the room.

"Doc," he shouted, "that damn machine of yours is at it again."

Dr. Kingsley turned and lumbered out, shouting back at them.

"Come along. Never mind the suits."

They ran behind him as he lumbered along. Through what obviously were the laboratory's living quarters, through a tiny kitchen that smelled of boiling coffee, into a workroom bare of everything except a machine that stood in one corner. A red light atop the machine was blinking rapidly.

The machine was a wonder in complexity, a spidery confusion of tubes and wires, an elaborate network of metal parts.

Dr. Kingsley lowered his huge frame into a chair before it, lifted a domed helmet and set it on his head. A pencil lay beside a pad of paper and he clutched at it, poised it over the pad as if to write. But the pencil remained poised and lines of concentration deepened in Kingsley's face. His left hand went up to the helmet and twisted knobs and dials.

Gary watched in amazement.

It must be over this contraption that Kingsley was receiving his mysterious messages. But he seemed to be having trouble. The message apparently wasn't coming in right.

The red light went dead and the doctor snatched the helmet from his head.

"Nothing again," he said, swinging about in his chair.

He rose slowly and there were lines of disappointment on his face, but his voice boomed as jovially as ever.

He flipped a hand at Tommy Evans.

"Meet Evans," he said. He introduced them in turn.

"Newspaper folks," he explained. "Out writing up the Solar System. Doing a good job of it, too. The last supply ship brought some *Evening Rockets*. Read your articles about the moons of Jupiter. Mighty interesting."

He lumbered back to the kitchen and poured coffee while they took off their spacesuits.

"I suppose," he said, "you're wondering what it's all about."

Gary nodded. "My office notified me," he replied. "Asked me to get a story about it. I hope you can help me out."

Dr. Kingsley sipped at a steaming cup.

"Not much to tell," he said. "And a lot of it is off the record stuff. Afraid there isn't any story . . . yet."

Evans laughed shortly. "Don't be that way, doc," he said. "You know you've got plenty to tell him. Go ahead and spill it. He'll keep out what you say is off the record."

Dr. Kingsley looked questioningly at Gary.

"Whatever you say is off the record, is off the record," Gary told him.

"There's so much of it," rumbled the doctor, "that sounds like sheer dream stuff."

"Hell," said Evans, "there always is in everything new. My ships sound like it, too. But the thing will work, I know it will."

Kingsley perched himself on a heavy kitchen chair.

"It started more than a year ago," he said. "We were studying the cosmics. Elusive things, those rays. Men have studied them for about five thousand years and they still don't know as much about them as you think they would after all that time. We thought at first that we'd made a really astounding discovery, for our instruments, used on top of the building, showed that the rays came in definite patterns. Not only that, but they came in definite patterns at particular times. We developed new equipment and learned more about the pattern. We learned that it occurred only when Pluto had rotated into such a position that this particular portion of the planet was facing the Great Nebula in Andromeda. We learned that the pattern, besides having a certain fixed physical structure, also had a definite time structure, and that the intensity of the bombardment always remained the same. In other words, the pattern never varied as to readings; it occurred at fixed intervals whenever we directly faced the Great Nebula, and the intensity varied very slightly, showing an apparent constant source of energy operating at specific times. In between those times our equipment registered the general haphazard behavior one would expect in cosmic rays."

The doctor rumbled on: "The readings had me down. Cosmic simply shouldn't behave that way. There never had been any instance of their behaving that way at any time before. Of course, this was the first thorough investigation far from the Sun's interfering magnetic fields. But why should they behave in that manner only when we were broadside to the Great Nebula?

"My two assistants and I worked and studied and theorized and it finally came down to just one thing. The things we were catching with our instruments weren't cosmic rays at all. They were something else. Something new. Some strange impulse coming to us from outer space. Almost like a signal. Like something or someone or God-knows-what was signaling to someone or something stationed here on Pluto. We romanticized a bit. We toyed with the idea of signals coming from another galaxy, for you know the Great Nebula is an exterior galaxy, a mighty star system, some nine hundred million light years across intergalactic space.

"But that was just imagining. There was nothing to support it in the light of factual evidence. We still aren't sure what it's all about, although we know a great deal more now than we did then.

"The facts we did gather, you see, indicated that whatever we were receiving must be definite signals, must originate within some sort of intelligence. Some intelligence, you see, that would know just when and where to send them. But there was the problem of distance. Just suppose for a moment that they were coming from the Great Nebula. It takes light almost a billion years to reach us from the Nebula. While it is very probable that the speed of light can be far exceeded, there is little reason to believe at present than anything could be so much faster than light that signaling could be practical across such enormous space. Unless, of course, the matter of time were mixed up a little, and when you get into that you have a problem that takes more than just a master mind. There was just one thing that would seem a probable answer . . . that if the signals were being sent from many light years distant, they were being routed through something other than all that space. Perhaps through another continuum of space-time, through what you might call, for the want of a better term, the fourth dimension."

"Doctor," said Herb, "you got me all balled up."

Dr. Kingsley's chuckle rumbled through the room.

"It had us that way, too," he said. "And then we figured maybe we were getting pure thought. Thought telepathed across the light years of unimaginable space. Just what the speed of thought would be no one could even guess. It might be instantaneous . . . it might be no faster than the speed of light . . . or any speed in between the two. But we do know one thing: that the signals we are receiving are the projection of thought. Whether they come straight through space or whether they travel through some short cut, through some manipulation of space-time frames, I do not know and I probably will never know.

"It took us months to build that machine you saw in the other room. Briefly, it picks up the signals, translates them from the pure energy of thought into actual thought, into symbols our mind can read. We also developed a method of sending our own thoughts back, of communicating with whatever or whoever it is that is trying to talk with Pluto. So far we haven't been successful in getting an entire message across. However, apparently we have succeeded in advising whoever is sending out the messages that we are trying to answer, for recently the messages have changed, have a note of desperation, frantic command, almost a pleading quality."

He brushed his coat sleeve across his brow.

"It's all so confusing," he confessed.

"But," asked Herb, "why would anyone send messages to Pluto? Until men came here, there was no life on the planet. Just a barren planet, without any atmosphere, too cold for anything to live. The tail end of creation."

Kingsley stared solemnly at Herb.

"Young man," he said, "we must never take anything for granted. How are we to say there never was life or intelligence on Pluto? How do we know that a great civilization might not have risen and flourished here aeons ago? How do we know that an expeditionary force from some far-distant star might not have come here and colonized this outer planet many years ago?"

"It don't sound reasonable," said Herb.

Kingsley gestured impatiently.

"Neither do these signals sound reasonable," he rumbled. "But there they are. I've thought about the things you mention. I am damned with an imagination, something no scientist should have. A scientist should just plug along, applying this bit of knowledge to that bit of knowledge to arrive at something new. He should leave the imagination to the philosophers. But I'm not that way. I try to imagine what might have happened or what is going to happen. I've imagined a mother planet groping out across all space, trying to get in touch with some long-lost colony here on Pluto. I've imagined someone trying to re-establish communication with the people who lived here millions of years ago. But it doesn't get me anywhere."

Gary filled and lit his pipe, frowning down at the glowing tobacco. Voices in space again. Voices talking across the void. Saying things to rack the human soul.

"Doctor," he said, "you aren't the only one who has heard thought from outer space."

Kingsley swung on him, almost belligerently. "Who else?" he demanded.

"Miss Martin," said Gary quietly, puffing at his pipe. "You haven't heard Miss Martin's story yet. I have a hunch that she can help you out."

"How's that?" rumbled the scientist.

"Well, you see," said Gary, softly, "she's just passed through a thousand years of mind training. She's thought without ceasing for almost ten centuries."

Kingsley's face drooped in amazement.

"That's impossible," he said.

Gary shook his head. "Not impossible at all. Not with suspended animation."

Kingsley opened his mouth to object again, but Gary hurried on. "Doctor," he asked, "do you remember the historical account of the Caroline Martin who refused to give an invention to the military board during the Jovian war?"

"Why, yes," said Kingsley. "Scientists have speculated for many years on just what it was she found—"

He started out of his chair.

"Caroline Martin!" he shouted.

He looked at the girl.

"Your name is Caroline Martin, too," he whispered huskily.

Gary nodded. "Doctor, this is the woman who refused to give up that secret a thousand years ago."

Chapter Five

DR. KINGSLEY glanced at his watch.

"It's almost time for the signals to begin," he said. "In another few minutes we will be swinging around to face the Great Nebula. If you looked out you would see it over the horizon now."

Caroline Martin sat in the chair before the thought machine, the domed helmet settled on her head. All eyes in the room were glued on the tiny light atop the mechanism. When the signals started coming that light would blink its bright-red eye.

"Lord, it's uncanny," whispered Tommy Evans. He brushed at his face with his hand.

Gary watched the girl. Sitting there so straight, like a queen with a crown upon her head. Sitting there, waiting, waiting to hear something that spoke across a gulf that took light many years to span.

Brain sharpened by a thousand years of thought, a woman who was schooled in hard and simple logic. She had thought of many things out in the shell, she said, had set up problems and had worked them out. What were those problems she had thought about? What were the mysteries she had solved? She was a young, rather sweet-faced kid, who ought to like a good game of tennis, or a dance . . . and she'd thought a thousand years.

Then the light began to blink and Gary saw Caroline lean forward, heard the breath catch sharply in her throat. The pencil she had poised above the pad dropped from her fingers and fell onto the floor.

Heavy silence engulfed the room, broken only by the whistling of the breath in Kingsley's nostrils. He whispered to Gary: "She understands! She understands . . ."

Gary gestured him to silence.

The red light blinked out and Caroline swung around slowly in the chair. Her eyes were wide and for a moment she seemed unable to give voice to the words she sought.

Then she spoke. "They think they are contacting someone else," she said. "Some great civilization that must have lived here at one time. The messages come from far away. From even farther than the Great Nebula. The Nebula just happens to be in the same direction. They are puzzled that we do not answer. They know someone has been trying to answer. They're trying to help us to get through. They talked in scientific terms I could not understand ... something to do with the warping of space and time, but involving principles that are entirely new. They want something and they are impatient. It seems there is a great danger someplace. They think that we can help."

"Great danger to whom?" asked Kingsley.

"I couldn't understand," said Caroline.

"Can you talk back to them?" asked Gary. "Do you think you could make them understand?"

"I'll try," she said.

"All you have to do is think," Kingsley told her. "Think clearly and forcefully. Concentrate all that you can, as if you were trying to push the thought away from you. The helmet picks up the impulses and routes them through the thought projector."

Her slim fingers reached out and turned a dial. Tubes came to life and burned into a blue intensity of light. A soaring hum of power filled the tiny room.

The hum became a steady drone and the tubes were filled with a light that hurt one's eyes.

"She's talking to them now," thought Gary. "She is talking to them."

The minutes seemed eternities, and then the girl reached out and closed the dial. The hum of power receded, clicked off and was replaced by a deathly silence.

"Did they understand?" asked Kingsley, and even as he spoke the light blinked red again.

Kingsley's hand closed around Gary's arm and his harsh whisper rasped in Gary's ear.

"*Instantaneous!*" he said. "Instantaneous signals! They got her message and they are answering. That means the signals are routed through some extra-dimension."

Swiftly the red light blinked. Caroline crouched forward in the chair, her body tensed with what she heard.

The light blinked off and the girl reached up and tore the helmet off.

"It can't be right," she sobbed. "It can't be right."

Gary sprang forward, put an arm around her shoulder. "What's wrong?" he asked.

"Those messages," she cried. "They come from the very edge of all the universe . . . *from the farthest rim of exploding space!*"

Kingsley leaped to his feet.

"They are like the voices I heard before," she said. "But different, somehow. More kindly . . . but terrifying, even so. They think they are talking to someone else. To a people they talked to here on Pluto many years ago . . . I can't know how many, but it was a long, long time ago."

Gary shook his head in bewilderment and Kingsley rumbled in his throat.

"At first," Caroline whispered, "they referred to us by some term that had affection in it . . . actual kinfolk affection, as if there were blood ties between them and the things they were trying to talk to here. The things that must have disappeared centuries ago."

"Longer ago than that," Kingsley told her. "That the thought bombardment is directed at this spot would indicate the things they are trying to reach had established some sort of a center, perhaps a city, on this site. There are no indications of former occupancy. If anyone was ever here, every sign of them has been swept away. And here there is no wind, no weather, nothing to erode, nothing to blow away. A billion years would be too short a time—"

"But who are they?" asked Gary. "These ones you were talking to. Did they tell you that?"

She shook her head. "I couldn't exactly understand. As near as I could come, they called themselves the Cosmic Engineers. That's a very poor translation. Not sufficient at all. There is a lot more to it."

She paused as if to marshal a definition. "As if they were self-appointed guardians of the entire universe," she explained. "Champions of all things that live within its space-time frame. And something is threatening the universe. Some mighty force out beyond the universe . . . out where there's neither space nor time."

"They want our help," she said.

"But how can we help them?" asked Herb.

"I don't know. They tried to tell me, but the thoughts they used were too abstract. I couldn't understand entirely. A few clues here and there. They'll have to reduce it to simpler terms."

"We couldn't even get there to help them," said Gary. "There is no way in which we can reach the rim of the universe. We haven't yet gone to the nearest star."

"Maybe," suggested Tommy Evans, "we don't need to get there. Maybe we can do something here to help them."

The red light was blinking again. Caroline saw it and reached for the helmet, put it on her head. The light clicked out and her hand went out and moved a dial. Again the tubes lighted and the room trembled with the surge of power.

Dr. Kingsley was rumbling. "The edge of space. But that's impossible!"

Gary laughed at him silently.

The power was building up. The room throbbed with it and the blue tubes threw dancing shadows on the wall.

Gary felt the cold wind from space again, flicking at his face, felt the short hairs rising at the base of his skull.

Kingsley was jittery. And he was jittery. Who wouldn't be at a time like this? A message from the rim of space! From that inconceivably remote area where time and space still surged outward into that no-man's-land of nothingness . . . into that place where there was no time or space, where nothing had happened yet, where nothing had happened ever, where there was no place and no circumstance and no possibility of event that could allow anything to happen. He tried to imagine what would be there. And the answer was nothing. But what was nothing?

Many years ago some old philosopher had said that the only two conceptions which Man was capable of perceiving were time and space, and from these two conceptions he built the entire universe, of these two things he constructed the sum total of his knowledge. If this were so, how could one imagine a place where neither time nor space existed? If space ended, what was the stuff beyond that wasn't space?

Caroline was closing the dials again. The blue light dimmed and the hum of power ebbed off and stopped. And once again the red light atop the machine was blinking rapidly.

He watched the girl closely, saw her body tense and then relax. She bent forward, intent upon the messages that were swirling through the helmet.

Kingsley's face was puckered with lines of wonderment. He still stood beside his chair, a great bear of a man, his hamlike hands opening and closing, hanging loosely at his side.

Those messages were instantaneous. That meant one of two things: that thought itself was instantaneous or that the messages were routed through a space-time frame which shortened the distance, that, through some manipulation of the continuum, the edge of space might be only a few miles . . . or a few feet . . . distant. That, starting now, one might walk there in just a little while.

Caroline was taking off her helmet, pivoting around in her chair. They all looked at her questioningly and no one asked the question.

"I understand a little better now," she said. "They are friends of ours."

"Friends of ours?" asked Gary.

"Friends of everyone within the universe," said Caroline. "Trying to protect the universe. Calling for volunteers to help them save it from some outside danger . . . from some outside force."

She smiled at the circle of questioning faces.

"They want us to come out to the edge of the universe," she said, and there was a tiny quaver of excitement in her voice.

Herb's chair clattered to the floor as he leaped to his feet. "They want us . . ." he started to shout and then he stopped and the room swam in heavy silence.

Gary heard the rasp of breath in Kingsley's nostrils, sensed the effort that the man was making to control himself as he shaped a simple question . . . the question that any one of them would have asked.

"How do they expect us to get out there?" Kingsley asked.

"My ship is fast," Tommy Evans said, "faster than anything ever built before. But not that fast!"

"A space-time warp," said Kingsley, and his voice was oddly calm. "They must be using a space-time warp to communicate with us. Perhaps. . . ."

Caroline smiled at him. "That's the answer," she said. "A short cut. Not the long way around. Cut straight through the ordinary space-time world lines. A hole in space and time."

Kingsley's great fists were opening and closing again. Each time he closed them the knuckle bones showed white through the tight-stretched skin.

"How will we do it?" asked Herb. "There isn't a one of us in the room could do it. We play around with geosectors that we use to drive our ships and think we're the tops in progress. But the geosectors just warp space any old way. No definite pattern, nothing. Like a kid playing around in a mud puddle, pushing the mud this way or that. This would take control . . . you'd have to warp it in a definite pattern and then you'd have to make it stay that way."

"Maybe the Engineers," said Evans.

"That's it," nodded Caroline. "The Engineers can tell us. They know the way to do it. All we have to do is follow their instructions."

"But," protested Kingsley, "could we understand? It would involve mathematics that are way beyond us."

Caroline's voice cut sharply through his protest. "I can understand them," she replied, bitterly. "Maybe it will take a little while, but I can work them out. I've had . . . practice, you know."

Kingsley was dumfounded. "You can work it out?"

"I worked out new mathematical formulas, new space theories out in the ship," she said. "They're only theories, but they ought to work. They check in every detail. I went over them point by point."

She laughed, with just a touch of greater bitterness.

"I had a thousand years to do it," she reminded him. "I had lots of time to work them out and check them. I had to do something, don't you see? Something to keep from going crazy."

Gary watched her closly, marveling at the complete self-assurance in her face, at the clipped confidence of her words. Vaguely, he sensed something else, too. That she was leader here. That in the last few minutes she had clutched in her tiny hands the leadership of this band of men on Pluto. That not all their brains combined could equal hers. That she held mastery over things they had not even thought about. She had thought, she said, for almost a thousand years.

How long did the ordinary man have to devote to thought? A normal lifetime of useful, skilled, well-directed adult effort did not extend much beyond fifty years. One third of that was wasted in sleep, one sixth spent in eating and in relaxation, leaving only a mere twenty-five years to think, to figure out things. And then one died and all one's thoughts were lost. Embryonic thoughts that might, in just a few more years, have sprouted into well-rounded theory. Lost and left for someone else to discover if he could . . . and probably lost forever.

But Caroline Martin had thought for forty lifetimes, thought with the sharp, quick brain of youth, without interruption or disturbance. No time out for eating or for sleeping. She might have spent a year, or a hundred years, on one problem had she wished.

He shivered as he thought of it. No one could even vaguely imagine what she knew, what keys she had found out there in the dark of interplanetary space. And—she had started with the knowledge of that secret of immense power she had refused to reveal even when it meant eternal exile for her.

She was talking again, her words crisp and clipped, totally unlike the delightful companion that she could be.

"You see, I am interested in time and space, always have been. The weapon that I discovered and refused to turn over to the military board during the Jovian war was your geosector . . . but with a vast difference in one respect."

"You discovered the geosector, the principle of driving

a ship by space warp, a thousand years ago?" asked Kingsley.

She nodded. "Except that they wouldn't have used it for driving ships . . . not then. For Jupiter was winning and everyone was desperate. They didn't care how a ship was driven; what they wanted was a weapon."

"The geosector is no weapon," Kingsley declared flatly. "You couldn't use it near a planetary body."

"But consider this," said the girl. "If you could control the space warp created by the geosector, and if the geosector would warp time as well as space, then it would be a weapon, wouldn't it?"

Herb whistled. "I'd say it'd be a weapon," he said, "and how!"

"They wanted to train it on Jupiter," Caroline explained. "It would have blasted the planet into nothingness. It would have scattered it not only through space, but through time as well."

"But think of what it would have done to the solar system," ejaculated Kingsley. "Even if the space warp hadn't distorted space throughout the entire system, the removal of Jupiter would have caused all the other planets to shift their orbits. There would have been a new deal in the entire system. Some of the planets would have broken up, some of them might have been thrown into the Sun. There most certainly would have been earthquakes and tidal waves and tremendous volcanic action on the Earth."

The girl nodded.

"That's why I wouldn't turn it over to them. I told them it would destroy the system. They adjudged me a traitor for that and condemned me to space."

"Why," said Gary, "you were nine centuries ahead of all of them! The first workable geosector wasn't built until a hundred years ago."

Nine hundred years ahead to start with, and a thousand years to improve upon that start! Gary wondered if she wasn't laughing at them. If she might not be able to laugh at even the Cosmic Engineers. Those geosectors out on the *Space Pup* must have seemed like simple toys to her.

He remembered how he had almost bragged about them, and felt his ears go red and hot.

"Young lady," rumbled Kingsley, "it seems to me that you don't need any help from these Cosmic Engineers."

She laughed at him, a tinkling laugh like the chime of silver bells. "But I do," she said.

The red light blinked and she picked up the helmet once again. Excitedly, the others watched her. The poised pencil dropped to the pad and raced across the smooth white paper, making symbolic marks, setting up equations.

"The instructions," Kingsley whispered, but Gary frowned at him so fiercely that he lapsed into shuffling silence, his great hands twisting at his side, his massive head bent forward.

The red light blinked out and Caroline snapped on the sending unit and once again the room was filled with the mighty voice of surging power and the flickering blue shadows danced along the walls.

Gary's head swam at the thought of it . . . that slim wisp of a girl talking across billions of light-years of space, talking with things that dwelt out on the rim of the expanding universe. Talking and understanding . . . but not perfectly understanding, perhaps, for she seemed to be asking questions, something about the equations she had written on the pad. The tip of her pencil hovered over the paper as her eyes followed along the symbols.

The hum died in the room and the blue shadows wavered in the white light of the fluorescent tube-lights. The red light atop the thought machine was winking.

The pencil made corrections, added notes and jotted down new equations. Never once hesitating. Then the light blinked off and Caroline was taking the helmet from her head.

Kingsley strode across the room and picked up the pad. He stood for long minutes, staring at it, the pucker of amazement and bafflement growing on his face.

He looked questioningly at the girl.

"Do you understand this?" he rasped.

She nodded blithely.

He flung down the pad. "There's only one other person in the system who could," he said. "Only one person who even remotely could come anywhere near knowing what it's all about. That's Dr. Konrad Fairbanks, and he's in a mental institution back on Earth."

"Sure," yelled Herb, "he's the guy that invented three-way chess. I took a picture of him once."

They disregarded Herb. All of them were looking at Caroline.

"I understand it well enough to start," she said. "I probably will have to talk with them from time to time to get certain things straightened in my mind. But we can always do that when the time comes."

"Those equations," said Kingsley, "represent advanced mathematics of the fourth dimension. They take into consideration conditions of stress and strain and angular conditions which no one yet has been able to fathom."

"Probably," Caroline suggested, "the Engineers live on a large and massive world, so large that space would be distorted, where stresses such as are shown in the equations would be the normal circumstance. Beings living on such a world would soon solve the intricacies of dimensional space. On a world that large, gravity would distort space. Plane geometry probably couldn't be developed because there'd be no such a thing as a plane surface."

"What do they want us to do?" asked Evans.

"They want us to build a machine," said Caroline, "a machine that will serve as an anchor post for one end of a space-time contortion. The other end will be on the world of the Engineers. Between those two machines, or anchor posts, will be built up a short-cut through the billions of light-years that separate us from them."

She glanced at Kingsley. "We'll need strong materials," she said. "Stronger than anything we know of in the system. Something that will stand up under the strain of billions of light-years of distorted space."

Kingsley wrinkled his brow.

"I was thinking of a suspended electron-whirl," she said. "Have you experimented with it here?"

Kingsley nodded. "We've stilled the electron-whirl," he said. "Our cold laboratories offer an ideal condition for that kind of work. But that won't do us any good. I can suspend all electronic action, stop all the electrons dead in their tracks, but to keep them that way they have to be maintained at close to absolute zero. The least heat and they overcome inertia and start up again. Anything you built of them would dissolve as soon as it heated up, even a few degrees.

"If we could crystallize the atomic orbit after we had stopped it," he said, "we'd have a material which would be phenomenally rigid. It would defy any force to break it down."

"We can do it," Caroline said. "We can create a special space condition that will lock the electrons in their places."

Kingsley snorted. "Is there anything," he asked, "that you can't do with space?"

Caroline laughed. "A lot of things I can't do, doctor," she told him. "A few things I can do. I was interested in space. That's how I happened to discover the space-time warp principle. I thought about space out there in the shell. I figured out ways to control it. It was something to do while away the time."

Kingsley glanced around the room, like a busy man ready to depart, looking to see if he had forgotten anything.

"Well," he rumbled, "what are we waiting for? Let us get to work."

"Now, wait a second," interrupted Gary. "Do we want to do this? Are we sure we aren't rushing into something we'll be sorry for? After all, all we have to go on are the Voices. We're taking them on face value alone . . . and Voices don't have faces."

"Sure," piped up Herb, "how do we know they aren't kidding us? How do we know this isn't some sort of a cosmic joke? Maybe there's a fellow out there somewhere laughing fit to kill at how he's got us all stirred up."

Kingsley's face flushed with anger, but Caroline laughed.

"You look so serious, Gary," she declared.

"It's something to be serious about," Gary protested. "We are monkeying around with something that's entirely out of our line. Like a bunch of kids playing with an atom bomb. We might set loose something we wouldn't be able to stop. Something might be using us to help it set up an easy way to get at the solar system. We might be just pulling someone's chestnuts out of the fire."

"Gary," said Caroline softly, "if you had heard that Voice you wouldn't doubt. I know it's on the level. You see, it isn't a voice, really ... it's a thought. I know there's danger and that we must help, do everything we can. There are other volunteers, you know, other people, or other things, from other parts of the universe."

"How do you know?" asked Gary fiercely.

"I don't know how," she defended herself. "I just know. That's all. Intuition, perhaps, or maybe a background thought in the Engineer's mind that rode through with the message."

Gary looked around at the others. Evans was amused. Kingsley was angry. He looked at Herb.

"What the hell," said Herb. "Let's take a chance."

Just like that, thought Gary. A woman's intuition, the burning zeal of a scientist, the devil-may-care, adventuresome spirit of mankind. No reason, no logic ... mere emotion. A throwback to the old days of chivalry.

Once a mad monk had stood before the crowds and shook a sword in air and shrieked invective against another faith, and, because of this, Christian armies, year after year, broke their strength against the walls of eastern cities.

Those were the Crusades.

This, too, was a crusade. A Cosmic Crusade. Man again answering the clarion call to arms. Man again taking up the sword on faith alone. Man pitting his puny strength, his little brain against great cosmic forces. Man ... the damn fool ... sticking out his neck.

Chapter Six

A GHOSTLY machine was taking shape upon the hard, pitted, frozen surface of the field ... a crazy machine that glimmered weirdly in the half-light of the stars. A machine with mind-wrenching angles, with flashing prisms and spidery framework, a towering skeleton of a machine that stretched out spaceward.

Made of material in which the atomic motion had been stilled, it stood defiant against the most powerful forces of man or void. Anchored magnetically to the core of the planet, it stood firmly planted, a spidery, frail-appearing thing, but with a strength that would stand against the unimaginable drag of a cosmic space-time warp.

From it long cables snaked their way over the frozen surface to the laboratory power plant. Through those slender cables, their resistance lowered by the bitter cold, tremendous power loads could be poured into the strange machine.

"They're space-nuts," grumbled Ted Smith at Gary's elbow. "They're fixing to blow Pluto all to hell. I wish there was some way for me to get away from here before the fireworks start."

Herbs' voice crackled in Gary's helmet-phones, answering the complaint. "Shucks, there just won't nothing happen. That contraption looks more like something a kid would build with a tinker toy set than a machine. I can't see, for the life of me, how it'll ever work."

"I gave up long ago," said Gary. "Caroline tried to explain it to me, but I guess I'm just sort of dense. I can't make head or tail of it. All I know is that it's supposed to be an anchor post, a thing that will help the Engineers set up this space warp of theirs and after it is set up will operate to hold it in position."

"I never did set any stock in that Engineer talk," Ted told him, "but there's been something I've been wanting to tell you two. Haven't been able to catch you, you've been so busy. But I wanted to tell you about it, for you're the only two who haven't gone entirely star-batty."

"What is it?" Gary asked.

"Well, you know," said Ted, "I don't attach much meaning to it, but it does seem kind of funny. A few days ago I sneaked out for a walk. Against orders, you know. Not supposed to get out of sight of the settlement. Too many things can happen here.

"But, anyhow, I went for a walk. Out along the mountains and over the carbon dioxide glacier and down into the little valley that lies just over the shoulder of the glacier."

He paused dramatically.

"You found something there?" asked Gary.

"Sure did," declared Ted proudly. "I found some ruins. Chiseled white stone. Scattered all over the valley floor. As if there had been a building there at one time and somebody had pulled it down stone by stone and threw the stones around."

"Sure it wasn't just boulders or peculiar rock formations?" asked Gary.

"No, sir," said Ted, emphatically. "There were chisel marks on those stones. Workmen had dressed them at some time. And all of it was white stone. You show me any white stone around here."

Gary understood what the radio operator meant. The mountains were black, black as the emptiness of space. He turned his head to stare at those jagged peaks that loomed over the settlement, their spearlike points faintly outlined against the black curtain of the void.

"Say," said Herb, "that sounds as if what the Engineers said about someone else living here at one time might be true."

"If Ted found building stone, that's exactly what it means," Gary asserted. "That would denote a city of some kind, intelligence of some kind. It takes a certain degree of culture to work stone."

"But," argued Herb, "how could anyone have lived here? You know that Pluto cooled quick, lost its lighter gases in a hurry. Its oxygen and carbon dioxide are locked up in snow and ice. Too cold for any life."

"I know all that," Gary agreed, "but it seems we can't be too sure of anything in this business. If Ted is right, it means the Engineers were right on at least one point where we all were wrong. It sort of gives a man more faith in what is going on."

"Well," said Ted, "I just wanted to tell you. I was going to go out there again some day and look around, but since then I've been too busy. Ever since you sent that story out, space has been full of messages . . . governmental stuff, messages from scientists and cranks. Don't give a man no time to himself at all."

As the radio man walked back to his shack, Gary looked toward the laboratory. Two space-suited figures were coming out of the main lock.

"That's Caroline and Kingsley," said Herb. "They've been up there to talk to the Engineers again. Got stuck on something. Wanted the Engineers to explain it to them."

"Looks to me like it's about finished," said Gary. "Caroline told me she didn't know just how much longer it would take, but she had hopes of getting it into working order in another day or two. Tommy's gone without sleep the last twenty hours, working to get his ship in tip-top shape. They've gone over the thing from control panel to rocket tubes."

"What I'd like to know," said Herb, irritably, "is just how we're going to use the ship in getting out to where the Engineers are."

"Those are instructions," said Gary. "Instructions from the Engineers. We don't dare do anything around here unless they say it's all right."

The space-suited figures were coming rapidly down the path to the space-field. Gary hailed them as they came nearer. "Find out what was wrong?" he asked.

Kingsley's voiced boomed at him. "Several things wrong," he declared. "This ought to put it in working shape."

The four of them advanced on the machine. Gary fell into step with Caroline and looked at the girl's face through her helmet visor. "You look fagged out," he said.

"I am tired," she confessed. They walked a few steps. "We had so much to do," she said, "and apparently so little time to do it in. The Engineers sound as if they are getting desperate. They seem to think the danger is very near."

"What I can't figure out," Gary told her, "is what we are going to do when we get there. They seem to be head and shoulders over us in scientific knowledge. If *they* can't work it out, I don't see how we can help them."

Her voice was full of weariness as she answered him.

"Neither do I," she said, "but they seemed so excited when they found out who we were, when I described our solar system to them and told them that the race had originated on the third planet. They asked so many questions about what kind of beings we were. It took a lot of explaining to get across the idea that we were protoplasmic creatures, and when they finally understood that they seemed even more excited."

"Maybe," suggested Gary, "protoplasmic beings are a rarity throughout the universe. Maybe they never heard of folks like us before."

She wheeled on him. "There's something funny about it all, Gary. Something funny about how anxious they are for us to come, how insistent they are in trying to find out so much about us . . . the extent of our science and our past history."

He thought he detected a quaver of fear in her voice. "Don't let it get you," he said. "If it gets too funny, we can always quit. We don't have to play their game, you know."

"No," she said, "we can't do that. They need us, need us to help them save the universe. I'm convinced of that."

She stepped quickly forward to help Kingsley.

"Hand me that hammer," said Kingsley's voice, and Gary stooped down, picked up the heavy hammer from the base of the machine and handed it to the scientist.

"Hell," complained Herb, "that's all we've done for days now. We've handed you wrenches and hammers and pins and bolts until I see them in my sleep."

Kingsley's chuckle sounded in their helmets as he swung the hammer against a crossbar, driving it into the mechanism at a slightly different angle.

Gary craned back his neck and gazed up the spiraling, towering height of the machine, out beyond into the blackness of space, studded with cruel-eyed stars. Out there, somewhere, was the rim of space. Out there, somewhere, a race of beings who called themselves the Cosmic Engineers were fighting a great danger which threatened the universe. He tried to imagine such a danger . . . a danger that would be a threat to that mighty bowl of matter and energy men called the universe, a living, expanding thing enclosed by curving time and space. But his brain swam with the bigness of the thought and he gave it up. It was entirely too big to even think about.

Tommy Evans was coming across the field from the hangar. He hailed them joyously. "The old tub is ready any time you are," he shouted.

Kingsley straightened from adjusting a series of prisms set around the base of the machine. "We're ready now," he said.

"Well, then," said Herb, "let us get going."

Kingsley stared out into space. "Not yet," he said. "We're swinging out of direct line with the Engineers. We'll wait until the planet rotates again. We can't hold the warp continuously. If we did, the rotation of Pluto would twist it out of shape. The machine, once the warp is set up, will act automatically, establishing the warp when it swings into the right position and maintaining it through forty-five degrees of Pluto's rotation."

"What happens," asked Gary, "if we can't complete the trip from here to the edge of the universe before Pluto travels that forty-five degrees? We might roll out of the warp and find ourselves marooned thousands of light-years between galaxies."

"I don't know," said Kingsley. "I'm trusting the Engineers."

"Sure," said Herb, "we're all trusting the Engineers. I hope to Heaven they know what they're doing."

Together the five of them trudged up the path to the main lock of the laboratory. "Something to eat," said Kingsley, "and a good sleep and we'll be starting out. All of us are pretty tuckered now."

In the little kitchen they crowded around the table, gulping steaming coffee and munching sandwiches. Beside Kingsleys' plate was a sheaf of spacegrams that Ted had brought up for him to read. Kingsley leafed through them irritably.

"Cranks," he rumbled. "Hundreds of them. All with ideas crazier than the one we have. And the biggest one of them all is the government. Imagine the government forbidding us to go ahead with our work. Orders to desist!" He snorted. "Some damn law that the Purity league got passed a hundred years or more ago and still standing on the statutes. Gives the government power to stop any experiment which might result in the loss of life or the destruction of property."

"The Purity league is still going pretty strong," said Gary, "although it works mostly undercover now. Too much politics mixed up in it."

He dug into the pocket of his coat and hauled forth a sheet of yellow paper. "I got this a while ago," he said. "I plain forgot about it until now. Too much other excitement."

He handed the sheet to Kinsgley. The folded paper crackled crisply as Kingsley unfolded it. It was a sheet off the teletype in the *Space Pup* and it read:

> NELSON. ABOARD SPACE PUP ON PLUTO. SOLAR GOVERNMENT ORDERED OUT SOLAR POLICE SECRETLY TWO DAYS AGO TO ENFORCE ORDER TO STOP EDGE OF UNIVERSE TRIP. THIS IS A WARNING. KEEP YOUR NOSE OUT OF WHATEVER IS GOING ON.

Kingsley crumpled the message savagely in his fist. "When did you get this?" he thundered.

"Just a couple of hours ago," said Gary. "It will take them days to get here."

"We'll be gone long before they even sight Pluto," Tommy said, his words mumbled through a huge bite of sandwich.

"That's right," agreed Kingsley, "but it makes me sore. The damn government always meddling in other people's affairs. Setting itself up as a judge and jury. Figuring it never can be wrong." He growled wickedly at the sandwich he held in one mighty fist, bit at it viciously.

Herb looked around the room. "This being sort of a farewell banquet," he said, "I sure wish we had something to drink. We ought to drink a toast to the Solar System before we leave it. We ought to make it just a little like a celebration."

"We'd have something to drink if you hadn't been so clumsy with that Scotch," Gary reminded him.

"Hell," retorted Herb, "that would have been gone long ago, with you making a pass at it every time you came in reach." He sighed and tilted his coffee cup against his face.

Kingsley's laugh thundered through the room. "Wait a minute, boys," he said. He went to a cupboard and removed a double row of canned vegetables from a shelf. A quart bottle filled with amber liquor was revealed. He set it on the table.

"Wash out your coffee cups," he said. "We haven't any glasses."

The liquor splashed into the coffee cups and they stood to drink a toast.

The telephone in the next room rang.

They set down their cups and waited as Kingsley went to answer it. They heard his roar of excitement and quick fire of rumbling questions. Then he was striding back into the room.

"My assistant, Jensen, was up in the observatory just now," he shouted at them. "He spotted five ships coming in, only a few hours out. Police ships!"

Herb had lifted his cup and now with a clatter it fell to the table, breaking. The liquor dripped to the floor.

Gary flared at him. "What's the matter with you?" he asked. "You get the shakes every time you get anywhere near a drink."

"That message Gary got," Tommy was saying. "There must have been something wrong. Maybe the ships were out near Neptune when they were ordered out here."

"What would they be doing out near Neptune?" snapped Herb.

Tommy shrugged. "Police ships are always snooping around," he said. "You find them everywhere."

They stared at one another in a deathly silence.

"They can't stop us now," whispered Caroline. "They just can't."

"There's still a couple of hours before the space warp contact with the Engineers would be broken if we set it

55

up now," said Tommy. "Maybe we could make it. The ship is ready."

"Ask the Engineers," said Gary. "Find out how soon they can get us there."

Kingsley's voice thundered commands. "Caroline," he was shouting, "get the Engineers! Find out if it would be safe to start now. Tommy, get out the spaceship! The rest of you grab what stuff we need and get down to the field."

The room was a swirl of action. All of them were rushing for the door.

Kingsley was at the telephone, talking to Andy. "Get the hangar doors open," he was shouting. "Warm up the tubes. We're taking off."

Through the thud of running feet, the rumbling of Kingsley's voice, came the high-pitched drone of the thought-machine sending set. Caroline was talking to the Engineers.

More snatches of telephone conversation. Kingsley talking with Jensen now. "Get down to the power house. Stand ready to give us all the juice you have. The leads will carry everything you can throw into them. We'll need a lot of power."

Gary was struggling into his space-armor when Caroline came into the room.

"We can make it," she shouted excitedly. "The Engineers say we'll be there in almost no time at all. Almost instantaneous."

Gary held her spacesuit for her while she clambered into it, helped her fasten down the helmet. Kingsley was puffing and grunting, hauling the space-armor over his portly body.

"We'll beat them," he was growling. "Damn them, we'll beat them yet! No government is going to tell me what I can do and what I can't do."

Out of the air lock, they raced down the path to the field. In the center of the field reared the ghostly machine, like a shimmering skeleton standing guard over the bleakness that was Pluto. As he ran, Gary glanced up and out into space.

A voice sang in his brain, the voice of his own thoughts: "We're coming! Hang on, you Engineers! We're on our way. Little puny man is coming out to help you. Mankind is marching to another crusade! To the biggest crusade he has ever known!"

Tommy Evans' mighty ship was at the far end of the field, a gleaming thing of silver, with the tubes a dull red, preheated to stand the sudden flare of rocket blasts in the deadly cold of Pluto's surface.

Yes, thought Gary, another crusade. But a crusade without weapons. Without even knowing who the enemy might be. Without a definite plan of campaign. With no campaign at all. With just an ideal and the sound of bugles out in space. But that was all man had needed ... ever. Just an ideal and the blaring of bugles.

Caroline cried out in wonder, almost in fear, and Gary glanced toward the center of the field.

The machine was gone! Where it had stood there was nothing, no faintest hint it had ever stood there. Just empty field and nothing else.

"Jensen turned on the power!" Kingsley shouted. "The machine is warped into another dimension. The road is open to the Engineers."

Gary pointed out into space. "Look," he yelled.

A faint, shimmering circle of light lay far out into the black depths. A slow wheel of misty white. A nebulous thing that hadn't been there before.

"That's where we go," said Kingsley, and Gary heard the man's breath whistling through his teeth. "That's where we go to reach the Engineers."

Chapter Seven

Tommy's nimble fingers flew over the rocket bank, set up a take-off pattern. His thumb tripped the firing lever and the ship surged up from the field with the thunder of the rocket blasts shuddering through its frame-work.

"Hit dead center," warned Kingsley and Tommy nodded grimly.

"Don't you worry," he snorted. "I will hit it."

"I'd like to see the look on the face of them dumb cops when they reach Pluto and find us gone," said Herb. "Thought they were putting over a fast one on us."

"It'll be all right if they don't set down right into that machine down there," Gary declared. "If they did that something would happen to them . . . and happen awful fast."

"I told Ted to warn them away from it," Kingsley said. "I don't think they'd hurt the machine, but they would sure get messed up themselves. They may try to destroy it, and if they do, they're in for a real surprise. Nothing could do that." He chuckled. "Stilled atomic-whirl and rigid space-curvature," he said. "There's material for you!"

The ship lanced swiftly through space, heading for that wheeling circle of misty light.

"How far away would it be?" Gary asked and Kingsley shook his head.

"Not too far," he said. "No reason for it being too far away."

They watched it through the vision plate, saw the wheel of light expand, become a great spinning, frosty rim that filled the plate and in its center a black hole like a hub.

Tommy set up a corrective pattern and tripped the firing lever. The cross-hairs on the destination panel bore dead center on the night-black hub.

The wheel of light flared out, the hub became bigger and blacker, a hole in space . . . as if one were looking through it into space, but into a space where there were no stars.

The light disappeared. Just the black hub remained, filling the vision plate with inky blackness. Then the ship was flooded with that same blackness, a cloying, heavy blackness that seemed pressing in upon them.

Caroline cried out softly and then choked back the cry, for the blackness was followed almost instantly by a flood of light.

The ship was diving down toward a city, a monstrous city that jerked Gary's breath away. A city that piled height on height, like gigantic steps, with soaring towers that pointed at them like Titan fingers. A solid, massive city of gleaming white stone and square, utilitarian lines, a city that covered mile on mile of land, so that one could see no part of the planet that bore it, the city stretching from horizon to horizon.

Three suns blazed in the sky; one white, two a misty blue, all three pouring out a flood of light and energy that, Gary realized, would have made Sol seem like a tiny candle.

Tommy's fingers flew over the rocket banks, setting up a braking pattern. But even as he did, the speed of the ship seemed to slow, as if they were driving into a soft, but resistant cushion.

And in their brains rang a voice of command, a voice telling them to do nothing, that they and their ship would be brought down to the city in safety. Not so much like words as if each one of them had thought the very thought, as if each one of them knew exactly what to do.

Gary glanced at Caroline and saw her lips shape a single word. "Engineers."

So it hadn't been a nightmare after all. There really were a people who called themselves the Cosmic Engineers. There really was a city.

The ship still plunged downward, but its speed was slowing and now Gary realized that when first they had seen this pile of stone beneath them they had been many miles away. In comparison to the city, they and their ship were tiny things . . . little things, like ants crawling in the shadow of a mountain.

Then they were within the city, or at least its upper portion. The ship flashed past a mighty spire of stone and swung into its shadow. Below them they saw new details of the city, winding streets and broad parkways and boulevards, like tiny ribbons fluttering in the distance. A city that could thrill one with its mere bigness. A city which would have put a thousand New Yorks to shame. A city that dwarfed even the most ambitious dreams of mankind. A million of Man's puny cities piled into one. Gary tried to imagine how big the planet must be to bear such a city, but there was no use of thinking, for there was no answer.

They were dropping down toward one of the fifth tiers of buildings, down and down, closer and closer to the massive blocks of stone. So close now that their vision was cut off, and the terrace of the tier seemed like a broad, flat plain.

A section of the roof was opening, like a door opening outward into space. The ship, floating on an even keel, drifted gently downward, toward that yawning trap door. Then they were through the door, with plenty of room to spare, were floating quietly down between walls of delicate pastel hues.

The ship settled with a gentle bump and was still. They had arrived at their destination.

"Well, we're here," said Herb. "I wonder what we're supposed to do."

As if in answer to his question, the voice came again, the voice that was not a voice, but as if each person were thinking for himself.

It said: "This is a place we have prepared for you. You will find the gravity and the atmosphere and the surroundings natural to yourselves. You will need no space armor, no artificial trappings of any sort. Food is waiting you."

They stared at one another in amazement.

"I think," said Herb, "that I will like this place. Did you hear that? Food? I trust there's also drink."

"Yes," said the voice, "there is drink."

Herb's jaw dropped.

Tommy stepped out of the pilot's chair. "I'm hungry," he said. He strode to the inner valve of the air lock and spun the wheel. The others crowded behind him.

They stepped out of the ship onto a great slab of stone placed in the center of a gigantic room. The stone, apparently, was merely there for the ship to rest upon, for the rest of the floor was paved in scintillating blocks of mineral that flashed and glinted in the light from the three suns pouring in through a huge, translucent skylight. The walls of the room were done in soft, pastel shades, and on the walls were hung huge paintings, while ringed about the ship was furniture, perfect rooms of furniture, but with no dividing walls. An entire household, of palatial dimension, set up in a single room.

A living room, a library, bedrooms and a dining room. A dining room with massive oaken table and five chairs, and upon the table a banquet to do justice to a king.

"Chicken!" cried Herb and the word carried a weight of awe.

"And wine," said Tommy.

They stared in amazement at the table. Gary sniffed. He could smell the chicken.

"Antique furniture," said Kingsley. "That stuff would bring a fortune back in the solar system. Mostly Chatterton . . . and it looks authentic. And beautiful pieces, museum pieces, every one. Thousand years old at least." He stared from piece to piece. "But how did they get it here?" he burst out.

Caroline's laughter rang through the room, a chiming, silver laughter that had a note of wild happiness in it.

"What's the matter?" demanded Tommy.

"I don't see anything funny," declared Herb. "Unless there is a joke. Unless that chicken really isn't chicken."

"It's chicken," Caroline assured him. "And the rest of the food is real, too. And so is that furniture. Only I didn't think of it as antique. You see, a thousand years ago that sort of furniture was the accepted style. That was the smartest sort of pieces to have in your home."

"But you?" asked Gary. "What did you have to do with it?"

"I told the Engineers," she said. "They asked me what we ate and I told them. They must have understood me far better than I thought. I told them the kind of clothes we wore and the kind of furniture we used. But, you see, the only things I knew about were out of date, things the people used a thousand years ago. All except the chicken. You still eat chicken, don't you?"

"And how," grinned Herb.

"Why," said Gary, "this means the Engineers can make anything they want to. They can arrange atoms to make any sort of material. They can transmute matter!"

Kingsley nodded. "That's exactly what it means," he said.

Herb was hurrying for the table.

"If we don't get there, there won't be anything left," Tommy suggested.

The chicken, the mashed potatoes and gravy, the wine,

the stuffed olives ... all the food was good. It might have come out of the kitchen of the solar system's smartest hotel only a few minutes before. After days of living on coffee and hastily slapped-together sandwiches, they did full justice to it.

Herb regarded with regret the last piece of chicken and shook his head dolefully.

"I just can't do it," he moaned. "I just can't manage any more."

"I never tasted such food in all my life," Kingsley declared.

"They asked me what we ate," Caroline said, "so I thought of all the things I like the best. They didn't leave out a single one."

"But where are the Engineers?" asked Gary. "We haven't seen a thing of them. We have seen plenty of what they have done and can do, but not one has showed himself."

Footsteps rasped across the floor and Gary swung around in his chair. Advancing toward them was something that looked like a man, but not exactly a man. It was the same height, had the same general appearance ... two arms, two legs, a man-shaped torso and a head. But there was something definitely wrong with the face; something wrong with the body, too.

"There's the answer to your question," said Tommy. "There's an Engineer."

Gary scarcely heard him. He was watching the Engineer intently as the creature approached. And he knew why the Engineer was different. Cast in human shape, he was still a far cry from the humans of the solar system, for the Engineer was a metal man! A man fashioned of metallic matter instead of protoplasm.

"A metal man," he said.

"That's right," replied Kingsley, and keen interest rather than wonderment was in his words. "This must be a large planet. The force of gravity must be tremendous. Protoplasm probably would be unable to stand up under its pull. We'd probably just melt down if the Engineers hadn't fixed up this place for us."

"You are right," said the metal man, but his mouth

didn't open, his facial expression didn't change. He was speaking to them as the voice had spoken to them back on Pluto and again as they had entered the city. The Engineer stopped beside the table and stood stiffly, his arms folded across his chest.

"Is everything satisfactory?" asked the Engineer.

It was funny, this way he had of talking. No sound, no change of expression, no gesture . . . just words burning themselves into one's brain, the imprint of thought thrust upon one's consciousness.

"Why, yes," said Gary, "everything is fine."

"Fine," shouted Herb, waving a drumstick. "Why, everything is perfect."

"We tried so hard to do everything just as you told us," said the Engineer. "We are pleased that everything is all right. We had a hard time understanding one thing. Those paintings on the wall. You said they were things you had and were used to and we wanted so much to make everything as you wanted it. But they were something we had never thought of, something we had never done. We are sorry that we were so stupid. They are fine things. When this trouble is over, we may make more of them. They are so very beautiful. How queer it was we hadn't thought of them."

Gary swung around and stared at the painting opposite the table. Obviously it was a work in oils and seemed a very fine one. It portrayed some fantastic scene, a scene with massive mountains in the background and strange twisted trees and waist-high grass and the glitter of a distant waterfall. A picture, Gary decided, that any art gallery would be proud to hang.

"You mean," he asked, "that these are the first pictures you ever painted?"

"We hadn't even thought of it before," said the Engineer.

They hadn't known of paintings before. No single Engineer had ever thought to capture a scene on canvas. They had never wielded an artist's brush. But here was a painting that was perfect in color and in composition, well balanced, pleasing to the eye!

"One thing about you fellows," said Tommy, "is that you will tackle anything."

"It was so simple," said the Engineer, "that we are ashamed we never thought of it."

"But this trouble," rumbled Kingsley. "This danger to the universe. You told us about it back on Pluto, but you didn't explain. We would like to know."

"That," said the Engineer, "is what I am here to tell you."

No change in the tone of the thoughts . . . no slightest trend of emotion. No change of expression on his face.

"We will do whatever we can to help," Kingsley told him.

"We are sure of that," said the Engineer. "We are glad that you are here. We were so satisfied when you said that you would come. We feel you can help us very, very much."

"But the danger," prompted Caroline. "What is the danger?"

"I will begin," said the Engineer, "with information that to us is very elemental, although I do not believe you know it. You had no chance to find it out, being so far from the edge of the universe. But we who have lived here so many years, found the truth long ago.

"This universe is only one of many universes. Only one of billions and billions of universes. We believe there are as many universes as there are galaxies within our own universe."

The Earthlings looked in astonishment at him. Gary glanced at Kingsley and the scientist seemed speechless. He was sputtering, trying to talk.

"There are over fifty billion galaxies within our universe," he finally said. "Or at least that is what our astronomers believe."

"Sorry to contradict," said the Engineer. "There are many more than that. Many times more than that."

"More!" said Kingsley, faintly for him.

"The universes are four-dimensional," said the Engineer, "and they exist within a five-dimensional inter-space, perhaps another great super-universe with the universes within it taking the place of the galaxies as they are related to our universe."

"A universe within a universe," said Gary, nodding his head. "And might it not be possible that this super-universe is merely another universe within an even greater super-universe?"

"That might be so," declared the Engineer. "It is a theory we have often pondered. But we have no way of knowing. We have so little knowledge . . ."

A little silence fell upon the room, a silence filled with awe. This talk of universes and super-universes. This dwarfing of values. This relegating of the universe to a mere speck of dust in an even greater place!

"The universes, even as the galaxies, are very far apart," the Engineer went on. "So very far apart that the odds against two of them ever meeting are almost incomprehensibly great. Farther apart than the suns in the galaxies, farther apart, relatively, than the galaxies in the universe. But entirely possible that once in eternity two universes will meet."

He paused, a dramatic silence in his thought. "And that chance has come," he said. *"We are about to collide with another universe."*

They sat in stunned silence.

"Like two stars colliding," said Kingsley. "That's what formed our solar system."

"Yes," said the Engineer, "like two stars colliding. Like a star once collided with your Sun."

Kingsley jerked his head up.

"You know about that?" he asked.

"Yes, we know about that. It was long ago. Many million years ago."

"How do you know about this other universe?" asked Tommy. "How could you know?"

"Other beings in the other universe told us," said the Engineer. "Beings that know much more in many lines of research than we shall ever know. Beings we have been talking to for these many years."

"Then you knew for many years that the collision would take place," said Kingsley.

"Yes, we knew," said the Engineer. "And we tried hard,

the two peoples. We of this universe and those of the other universe. We tried hard to stop it, but there seemed no way. And so at last we agreed to summon, each from his own universe, the best minds we could find. Hoping they perhaps could find a way . . . find a way where we had failed."

"But we aren't the best minds of the universe," said Gary. "We must be far down the scale. Our intelligence, comparatively, must be very low. We are just beginning. You know more than we can hope to know for centuries to come."

"That may be so," agreed the Engineer, "but you have something else. Or you may have something else. You may have a courage that we do not possess. You may have an imagination that we could not summon. Each people must have something to contribute. Remember, we had no art, we could not think up a painting; our minds are different. It is so very important that the two universes do not collide."

"What would happen," asked Kingsley, "if they did collide?"

"The laws of the five-dimensional inter-space," explained the Engineer, "are not the laws of our four-dimensional universe. Different results would occur under similar conditions. The two universes will not actually collide. They will be destroyed before they collide."

"Destroyed before they collide?" asked Kingsley.

"Yes," said the Engineer. "The two universes will 'rub,' come so close together that they will set up a friction, or a frictional stress, in the five-dimensional inter-space. Under the inter-space laws this friction would create new energy . . . raw energy . . . stuff that had never existed before. Each of the universes will absorb some of that energy, drink it up. The energy will rush into our universes in ever-increasing floods. Unloosed, uncontrollable energy. It will increase the mass energy in each universe, will give each a greater mass . . ."

Kingsley leaped to his feet, tipping over a coffee cup, staining the table cloth.

"Increase the mass!" he shouted. "But . . ."

Then he sat down again, sagged down, a strangely beaten man.

"Of course that would destroy us," he mumbled. "Presence of mass is the only cause for the bending of space. An empty universe would have no space curvature. In utter nothingness there would be no condition such as we call space. Totally devoid of mass, space would be entirely uncurved, would be a straight line and would have no real existence. The more mass there is, the tighter space is curved. The more mass there is, the less space there is for it to occupy."

"Flood the universe with energy from inter-space," the Engineer agreed, "and space begins curving back, faster and faster, tighter and tighter, crowding the matter it does contain into smaller space. We would have a contracting rather than an expanding universe."

"Throw enough of that new energy into the universe," Kingsley rumbled excitedly, "and it would be more like an implosion than anything else. Space would rush together. All life would be destroyed, galaxies would be wiped out. Existent mass would be compacted into a tiny area. It might even be destroyed if the contraction was so fast that it crushed the galaxies in upon each other. At the best, the universe would have to start all over again."

"It would start over again," said the Engineer. "There would be enough new energy absorbed by the universe for just such an occurrence as you have foreseen. The entire universe would revert to original chaos."

"And me without my life insurance paid," said Herb.

Gary snarled at him across the table.

Caroline leaned her elbows on the table and cupped her chin in her hands. "The problem," she said, "is to find out how to control that new energy if it does enter the universe."

"That is the problem," agreed the Engineer.

"Mister," said Gary, "if anyone can do it, this little lady can. She knows more about a lot of things than you do. I'll lay you a bet on that."

Chapter Eight

THE suits were marvelous things, flexible and with scarcely any weight at all, not uncomfortable and awkward like an ordinary spacesuit.

Herb admired his before he fastened down the helmet. "You say these things will let us walk around on your planet just as if we were at home?" he asked the Engineer.

"We've tried to make it comfortable for you here," the Engineer replied. "We hope you find them satisfactory. You came so far to help and we are so glad to see you. We hope that you will like us. We have tried so hard."

Caroline looked toward the Engineer curiously. There was a queer, vague undertone to all his thought-messages, an inexplicable sense of pleading, of desire for praise from her or from Kingsley. She shook her head with a little impatient gesture, but still that deep, less-than-half-conscious feeling was there. It made no sense, she told herself. It was just imagination. The thought-messages were pure thought, there was nothing to interpret them, nothing to give them subtle shades of meaning . . . no facial expression, no change of tone.

But that pleading note!

It reminded her suddenly—with a little mounting lump in her throat—of her bird dog, a magnificent mahogany-and-white Chesapeake retriever, dead these thousand years. Somehow she felt again as she used to feel when the dog had looked up at her after placing a recovered bird at her feet.

He was gone now, gone with all the world she'd known. Her ideas and her memories were magnificent antiques, museum pieces, in this newer day. But she felt that if, somehow, that dog could have been granted eternal life, he'd be searching for her still . . . searching, waiting, hungering for the return that never came. And rising in queerly mixed ecstasies of gladness and shyness if she ever came back to him again.

Kingsley spoke and the rising feeling snapped.

"Gravity suits," said Kingsley, almost bursting with excitement. "But even more than that! Suits that will let a man move about comfortably under any sort of conditions. Under any pressure, any gravity, in any kind of atmosphere."

"With these," Gary suggested, "we would be able to explore Jupiter."

"Sure," said Tommy, "that would be easy. Except for one little thing. Find a fuel that will take you there and take you out again."

"Hell," enthused Herb, "I bet the Engineers could tell us how to make that fuel. These boys are bell-ringers all around."

"If there is any way we can help you, anything you want, anything at all," declared the Engineer, "we would be so glad, so proud to help you."

"I bet you would at that," said Herb.

"Only a few of the denizens we called have arrived," said the Engineer. "More of them should have come. Others may be on their way. We are afraid . . ."

He must have decided not to say what was on his mind, for thought clicked off, broken in the middle of the sentence.

"Afraid?" asked Kingsley. "Afraid of what?"

"Funny," said Gary, almost to himself. "Funny they should be afraid of anything."

"Not afraid for ourselves," explained the Engineer. "Afraid that we may be forced to halt our work. Afraid of an interruption. Afraid someone will interfere."

"But who would interfere?" asked Caroline. "Who could possibly interfere in a thing like this? The danger is a common one. All things within the universe should unite to try to fight it."

"What you say is right," declared the Engineer. "So right that it seems impossible any could think otherwise. But there are some who do. A race so blinded by ambition and by hatred that they see in this approaching catastrophe an opportunity to wipe us out, to destroy the Engineers."

The Earthlings stood stock-still, shocked.

"Now, wait a second," said Gary slowly. "Let us understand this. You mean to say that you have enemies who would die themselves just for the satisfaction of knowing that you were destroyed, too?"

"Not exactly," said the Engineer. "Many of them would be destroyed, but a select few would survive. They would go back to the point where the universe must start again, back to the point where space and time would once more begin expanding. And, starting there, they would take over the new universe. They would shape it to fit their needs. They would control it. They would have complete dominion over it."

"But," cried Gary, "that is mad! Utterly mad. Sacrificing a present people, throwing away an entire universe for a future possibility."

"Not so mad," said Kingsley quietly. "Our own Earth history will furnish many parallels. Mad rulers, power-mad dictators ready to throw away everything for the bare feel of power . . . ready to gamble with the horrors of increasingly scientific and ruthless warfare. It almost happened on Earth once . . . back in 2896. The Earth was almost wiped out when one man yearned for power and used biological warfare in its most hideous form. He knew what the result would be, but that didn't stop him. Better, he reasoned, if there were no more than a thousand persons left alive, if he were the leader of that thousand. Nothing stopped him. The people themselves later stopped him . . . after he had done the damage . . . stopped him like the mad dog that he was."

"They hate us," said the Engineer. "They have hated us for almost a million years. Because we, and we alone, have stood between them and their dreams of universal conquest. They see us as the one barrier they must remove, the one obstacle in their way. They know they never can defeat us by the power of arms alone, cannot defeat us so utterly that we still cannot smash their plans to take over the universe."

"And so," said Gary, "they are perfectly willing to let

the collision of universes wipe you out, even if it does mean disaster and destruction for the most of them."

"They must be nuts," said Herb.

"You do not understand," protested the Engineer. "For many millions of years they have been educated with the dream of universal conquest. They have been so thoroughly propagandized with the philosophy that the state, the civilization, the race, is everything . . . that the individual does not count at all . . . that there is not a single one of them who would not die to achieve that dream. They glory in dying, glory in any sort of sacrifice that advances them even the slightest step toward their eventual goal."

"You said that some of them would survive even if the universe, as we know it, were destroyed," said Caroline. "How would they do that?"

"They have found a way to burst out of the universe," said the Engineer. "How to navigate the inter-space that exists outside the universe. They are more advanced in many sciences that we. If they wished, I have no doubt they could by themselves, with no aid at all, save us from the fate that is approaching."

"Perhaps," rumbled Kingsley, "a treaty could be arranged. A sort of eleventh-hour armistice."

The impersonal thought of the Engineer struck at them. "There can be no peace with them. No treaty. No armistice. For more than a million years they have thought and practiced war. Their every thought has been directed toward conquest. To them the very word 'peace' is meaningless. War is their natural state, peace an unnatural state. And they would not, in any event, in the remote chance that they might consider an armistice, consider it at this time when they have a chance to prevent us from saving the universe."

"You mean," asked Gary, horror in his voice, "that they actually want the universe destroyed? That they would fight you to prevent you from saving it?"

"That," said the Engineer, "is exactly what I mean. You understand so well."

"Do you expect them to attack soon?" asked Tommy.

"We do not know. They may attack at any time. We

are ready at all times. We know they will attack eventually."

"We must find a way," said Caroline. "We can't let them stop us! We must find a way!"

"We will find a way," rumbled Kingsley. "There has to be a way, and we'll find it."

"What do you call these rip-snorters you've been fighting all these years?" asked Herb.

"We call them the Hellhounds," said the Engineer, but that was not exactly what he meant. The thought brought together a certain measure of loathing mixed with fear and hatred. Hellhounds was the nearest the Earthlings could translate the thought.

"They can break through the time-space curve," said Caroline, musingly, "and they can travel in the fifth-dimensional inter-space." She flashed a look at Gary, a look filled with the flare of inspiration. "Perhaps," she said, "that is the answer. Perhaps that is what we should try to find the answer to."

"I don't know what you mean," said Gary, "but maybe you are right."

"The space-time curve would be rigid," said Kingsley. "Rigid and hard to unravel. Lines of stress and force that would be entirely new. That would take mathematical knowledge. That and tremendous power."

"The power of new energy," said Gary. "Perhaps the power of the energy the rubbing universes will create."

Kingsley stared at him as if he had struck him with an open hand. "You have it," he shouted. "You have it!"

"But we haven't got the energy," said Gary, bluntly.

"No," agreed Kingsley. "We'll have to get that first."

"And control it," said Caroline.

"Perhaps," suggested the Engineer, "we should go now. The others are waiting for us. They have come so far, many of them from greater distances than you."

"How many are there?" asked Gary.

"Only a few," said the Engineer, "so very few. Life is so seldom found throughout the universe. The universe does not care for life. I sometimes think life is merely a strange disease that should not be here at all, that it is some accidental arrangement of matter that has no right to be. The universe is so hostile to it that it would seem almost to be abnormal. There are so few places where it can take root and live."

"But throughout those billions of galaxies there must be many races," declared Kingsley.

"There may be many we do not know about," said the Engineer, "but very few that we can contact. It is so very hard to get in touch with them. And some of them would be useless to us, races that had developed along entirely different lines to achieve a different culture. Races that live without the application of any of the practical sciences. Races that are sunken in the welter of philosophy and thought. Races that have submerged themselves in aesthetics and are untrained in science. The only ones we could reach were those scientifically-minded races that could catch our message and could reply to us . . . and after that could build the apparatus that would bring them here."

"Hell," said Herb, "it takes all kinds of people to make a universe."

The Engineer led them through an air lock which opened from the room into a mighty corridor . . . a corridor that stretched away for inconceivable distances, a vast place that held a brooding sense of empty space.

The suits functioned perfectly. Gravity and pressure were normal and the suits themselves were far more comfortable than the spacesuits used back in the solar system.

Slowly they trudged down the hall behind the Engineer.

"How long did it take to build this city?" asked Gary.

"Many years," said the Engineer. "Since we came here."

"Came here?" asked Gary. "Then this isn't your native planet?"

"No," said the Engineer, but he did not offer to explain.

"Say," said Herb, "you didn't ask our names. You don't know who we are."

Gary thought he detected a faint semblance of dry humor in the answer of the Engineer.

"Names," he said. "You mean personal designations? I know who you are without knowing names."

"Maybe," said Herb, "but we can't read thoughts like you can. We got to have names." He trotted along at the heels of the Engineer. "Don't you fellows have names?" he asked.

"We are designated by numbers," said the Engineer. "Purely as a matter of record. The individual doesn't count so much here as he does where you came from."

"Numbers," said Herb. "Just like a penitentiary."

"If it is necessary for you to designate me," said the Engineer, "my number is 1824. I should have told you sooner. I am sorry I forgot."

They halted before a massive door and the Engineer sounded a high-pitched thought-wave that beat fantastically against their minds. The great door slid back into the wall and they walked into a room that swept away in lofty reaches of vast distances, with a high-vaulted ceiling that formed a sky-like cup above them.

The room was utterly empty of any sort of furniture. Just empty space that stretched away to the dim, far walls of soaring white. But in its center was a circular elevation of that same white stone, a dais-like structure that reared ten feet or more above the white-paved floor.

Upon the dais stood several of the Engineers and around them were grouped queer, misshapen things, nightmares snatched from some book of olden horrors, monstrosities that made Gary's blood run cold as he gazed upon them.

He felt Caroline's fingers closing on his arm. "Gary," her whisper was thin and weak, "what are they?"

"Those are the ones that we have called," said the Engineer. "The ones who have come so far to help us in our fight."

"They look like something a man would want to step on," said Herb, and there was a horrible loathing in his words.

Gary stared at them, fascinated by their very repulsiveness. Lords of the universe, he thought. These are the things that represent the cream of the universe's intelligence. These things that looked, as Herb had said, like something you would want to step on.

The Engineer was walking straight ahead, toward the wide, shallow steps that led up to the dais.

"Come on," rumbled Kingsley. "Maybe we look as bad to them."

They crossed the hall and tramped up the steps. The Engineer crossed to the other Engineers.

"These," he said, "are the ones who have come from the outer planet of the solar system we have watched so many years."

The Engineers looked at them. So did the other things. Gary felt his skin crawling under the scrutiny.

"They are welcome," came the thought-wave of one of the Engineers. "You have told them how glad we are to have them here?"

"I have told them," declared Engineer 1824.

There were chairs for the Earthlings. One of the Engineers waved an invitation to them and they sat down.

Gary looked around. They were the only ones who had chairs. The Engineers, apparently tireless, remained standing. Some of the other things stood, too. One of them stood on a single leg with his second leg tucked tight against his body—like a dreaming stork—except that he didn't look like a stork. Gary tried to classify him. He wasn't a bird or a reptile or a mammal. He wasn't anything a human being had ever imagined. Long, skinny legs, great bloated belly, head with unkempt hair falling over brooding, dead-fish eyes.

One of the Engineers began to speak.

"We have gathered here," said the thought-waves, "to consider ways and means of meeting one of the greatest dangers . . ."

Just like a political speaker back on Earth, thought Gary. He tried to make out which one of the Engineers was talking, but there was no facial expression, no movement of any sort which would determine which one of them the speaker might be. He tried to pick out Engineer 1824, but all the Engineers looked exactly alike.

The talk rumbled on, a smooth roll of thought explaining the situation that they faced, the many problems it presented, the need of acting at once.

Gary studied the other things about them, the loathsome, unnatural things that had been brought here from the unguessed depths of the universe. He shuddered and felt cold beads of sweat break out upon his body as he looked at them.

Several of them were immersed in tanks filled with liquids. One tank boiled and steamed as if with violent chemical action; another was cloudy and dirty-looking; another was clear as water and in it lurked a thing that struck stark terror into Gary's soul. Another was confined in a huge glass sphere through which shifted and swirled a poisonous-appearing atmosphere. Gary felt cold fingers touch his spine as he watched the sphere and suddenly was thankful for the shifting mists within it, for through them he had caught sight of something that he was certain would have shattered one's mind to look upon without the shielding swirl of fog within the glass.

In a small glass cage set upon a pedestal of stone were several writhing, grub-like things that palpitated disgustingly. Squatting on its haunches directly across from Gary was a monstrosity with mottled skin and drooling mouth, with narrow, slitted eyes and slimy features. He fastened his pinpoint gaze upon the Earthman and Gary quickly looked away.

Nothing resembled mankind, nothing except the Engineers. Here were things that were terrible caricatures of the loathsome forms of Earth life, other beings that bore not even the most remote resemblance to anything that mankind had ever seen or imagined.

Was this a fair sample of the intelligence the universe contained? Did he and Kingsley and Caroline appear as disgusting, as fearsome in the eyes as these other denizens of the universe as they appeared to his?

He shot a quick glance at Caroline. She was listening intently, her chin cupped in one hand, her eyes upon the Engineers. Just as well that way, he thought. She didn't see these other things.

The Engineer had stopped talking and silence fell upon the room. Then a new impulse of thought beat against Gary's brain, thought that seemed cold and cruel, thought that was entirely mechanistic and consciousless. He glanced swiftly around, trying to find who was speaking. It must, he decided, be the thing in the glass sphere. He could not understand the thought, grasped just vague impressions of atomic structures and mathematics that seemed to represent enormous pressure used to control surging energy.

The Engineer was talking again.

"Such a solution," he was saying, "would be possible on a planet such as yours, where an atmosphere many miles in depth, composed of heavy gases, creates the pressures that you speak of. While we can create such pressures artificially, we could not create or maintain them outside the laboratory."

"What the hell," asked Herb, "are they arguing about?"

"Shut up," hissed Gary, and the photographer lapsed into shamefaced silence.

The cold, cruel thought was arguing, trying to explain a point that Gary could only guess at. He looked at Caroline, wondering if she understood. Her face was twisted into tiny lines of concentration.

The cold stream of thought had stopped and another thought broke in, a little piping thought. Perhaps, thought Gary, one of the little slug-like creatures in the glass cage. Disgusting little things!

Gary looked at the mottled, droopy-eyed creature that squatted opposite him. It raised its head and in the beady eyes he imagined that he caught a glimmer of amusement.

"By the Lord," he said to himself, "he thinks it's funny, too."

This arguing of hideous entities! The piping thoughts of slimy things that should be wriggling through some stagnant roadside ditch back on the planet Earth. The cold thought of the brain-blasting thing that lived on a planet covered by miles of swirling gases. The pinpoint eyes of the being with the mottled skin.

Cosmic Crusade! He laughed to himself, deep in his throat. This wasn't the way he had imagined it. He had thought of gleaming ships of war, of stabbing rays, of might arrayed against might, a place where courage would be at a premium.

But there was nothing to fight. No physical thing. Nothing a man could get at. Another universe, a mighty thing of curving space and time . . . that was the enemy. A man simply couldn't do anything about a thing like that.

"This place," Herb whispered to him, "is giving me the creeps."

Chapter Nine

"WE CAN do it," said Caroline. She flicked a pencil against a sheet of calculations. "This proves it," she declared.

Kingsley bent over her shoulder to look at the sheet. "If you don't mind," he said, "would you lead me through it all again. Go slowly, please. I find it hard to grasp a lot of it."

"Kingsley," said Herb, "you're just an amateur. To get as good as she is you'd have to think for forty lifetimes."

"You embarrass me," she said. "It's very simple. It's really very simple."

"I'll say it's simple," said Tommy. "Just a little matter of bending space and time into a tiny universe. Wrapping it about a selected bit of matter and making it stay put."

"You could use it to control the energy," rumbled Kingsley. "I understand that well enough. When the universes begin to rub you could trap the incoming energy in an artificial universe. The energy would destroy that universe, but you'd have another ready for it. What I can't understand is how you form this artificial fourth-dimensional space."

"It isn't artificial," snapped Gary. "It's real . . . as real as the universe we live in. But it's made by human beings instead of by some law we have no inkling of."

He pointed at the sheet of calculations. "Perhaps the secret of all the universe is on that sheet of paper," he declared. "Maybe that's the key to how the universe was formed."

"Maybe," rumbled Kingsley, "and maybe not. There may be many ways to do it."

"One," said Gary, "is good enough for me."

"There's just one thing," said Caroline, "that bothers

me. We don't know anything about the fifth-dimensional inter-space. We can imagine that its laws are different from our own. Vastly different. But how do they differ? What kind of energy would be formed out there? What form would it take?" She looked from one to the other of them. "That would make a lot of difference," she declared.

"It would," agreed Kingsley. "It would make a lot of difference. It would be like setting a trap for some animal. You might set one for a rat and catch a bear . . . or the other way around."

"The Hellhounds know," said Tommy. "They know how to navigate in the inter-space."

"But they wouldn't tell us," said Gary. "They don't want the universe to be saved. They want it to be wrecked so they can build a new world out of the wreckage."

"It might be light, or matter, or heat, or motion, or it might be something that's entirely different," said Caroline. "It's not impossible it would be something else, some new fearful form of energy with which we are entirely unacquainted. Conditions would be just as different out in inter-space as fourth-dimensional conditions differ from our three-dimensional world."

"And to be able to control it we would have to have some idea as to what it is," said Kingsley.

"Or what it would become when it entered the hyperspace," said Gary. "It might be one kind of energy out there, an entirely different kind when it entered our universe."

"The people of the other universe don't seem to know," Tommy pointed out. "Even if they are the ones who found out about the universes drifting together. They don't seem to be able to find out too much about it."

Gary glanced around the laboratory, a mighty vaulted room that glowed with soft, white light . . . a room with gleaming tiers of apparatus, with mighty machines, great engines purring with tremendous power, uncanny structures that almost defied description.

"The funniest thing about the whole business," he declared, "is why the Engineers themselves can't make any progress. Why do they have to call us in? With all of this equipment, with the knowledge they already hold, it ought to be a cinch for them to do almost anything."

"There's something queer here," Herb declared. "I've been snooping around a bit and this city is enough to set you batty. There isn't any traffic in the streets. You can travel for hours and you don't see a single Engineer. No business houses, no theaters, no nothing. All the buildings are empty. Just empty buildings. A city of empty buildings." He puffed out his breath. "Like a city that was built and waiting for someone. Waiting for someone who never came."

Something akin to terror crossed Gary's mind. A queer, haunted feeling . . . a pity for those magnificent white buildings standing all untenanted.

"A city built for billions of people," said Herb. "And no one in it. Just a handful of Engineers. Probably not more than a hundred thousand altogether."

Kingsley was clenching and opening his fists again, rumbling in his throat.

"It does seem queer," he said, "that they never found the answer. With all their knowledge, all their scientific apparatus."

Gary looked at Caroline and smiled. A wisp of a girl. But one who could bend space and time until it formed a sphere . . . or, rather, a hypersphere. A girl who could mold space as she wanted it, who could play tricks with it, make it do what she wanted it to do. She could set up a tiny replica of the universe, a little private universe that belonged to her and no one else. No one before, he was certain, ever had dared to think of doing that.

He looked at her again, a swift, sure look that saw the square-cut chin, the high forehead, the braided raven strands about her head. Was Caroline Martin greater than the Engineers? Could she master a problem that they couldn't even touch? Was she, all unheralded, the master mind of the entire universe? Did the hope of the universe lie within her mind?

It seemed impossible. And yet, she had thought of time and space for nearly forty lifetimes. With nothing but a brain to work with, with no tools, no chance of experimentation—all alone, with nothing but her thoughts, she had solved the deep-shrouded mysteries of space and time. Never dreaming, perhaps, that such knowledge could be used to a certain purpose.

Metal feet scraped across the laboratory floor and Gary whirled to come face to face with Engineer 1824. The metal man had advanced upon them unawares.

His thought came to them, clear, calm, unhurried thought, devoid of all emotion, impersonal, yet with a touch of almost human warmth.

"I heard your thoughts," he said, "and I am afraid that you might think I meant to hear them. But I am very glad I did. You wonder why the Engineers brought you here. You wonder why the Engineers can't do this work unaided."

They stood guiltily, like schoolboys caught at some forbidden act.

"I will tell you," the thought went on, "and I hope you will understand. It is difficult to tell you. Hard to tell you, because we Engineers are full of pride. Conditions being different, we would never tell you."

It sounded like a confession, and Gary stared at the metal man in stricken surprise, but there was no sign of expression upon the metal face, no hint of thought within the glowing eyes.

"We are an old and tired people," said the Engineer. "We have lived too long. We have always been a mechanistic people and as the years went on we became even more so. We plod from one thing to another. We have no imagination. The knowledge that we have, the powers we hold, were inherited by us. Inherited from a great race, the greatest race that ever lived. We have added something to that knowledge, but so very little. So very, very little when you think of all the time that has passed away since it was handed to us."

"Oh!" cried Caroline and then put her hand up as if to cover her mouth, and it clanged against the quartz of the helmet. She looked at Gary and he saw pity in her eyes.

"No pity for us, please," said the Engineer. "For we are a proud people and have the right to be. We have kept an ancient trust and kept it well. We have abided by the heritage that is ours. We have kept intact the charge that was given us."

In the little silence Gary had a sense of ancient things, of old plays played out upon a stage that had dissolved in dust these many thousand years. A sense of an even greater race upon an even greater planet. An old, old heraldry carried down through cosmic ages by these metal men.

"But you are young," declared the Engineer. "Your race is young and unspoiled. You have fallen into no grooves. Your mind is free. You are full of imagination and initiative. I sensed it when I talked with you back in your own system. And that is what we need . . . that is what we must have. Imagination to grasp the problem that is offered. Imagination to peer around the corner. A dreaming contemplation of what is necessary to be done, and then the vigorous initiative to meet the challenge that the dream may bring."

Again a silence.

"That is why we are so glad to have you here," went on the Engineer. "That is why I know I can tell you what must be told."

He hesitated for a moment and a million fears speared at Gary's brain. Something that must be told! Something they hadn't known before. An even greater threat to face?

They waited breathlessly.

"You should know," said the Engineer, "but I almost fear to tell you. It is this: *Upon you, and you alone, must rest the fate of the universe. You are the only ones to save it.*"

"Upon us," cried Tommy. "Why, that is mad! You can't mean it!"

Kingsley's hands were clenched and the bearish rumble was rising in his throat. "What about those others?" he asked. "All those others you brought here, along with us?"

"I sent them back," declared the Engineer. "They were no help to us."

Gary felt the cold wind from space reach out and flick his face again. Man—and Man alone—stood between the universe and destruction. Little, puny Man. Man, with a body so delicate that he would be smashed to a bloody pulp if exposed unprotected to the naked gravity of this monstrous world. Little Man, groping toward the light, groping, feeling, not knowing where he went.

And then the blast of trumpets sounded in the air— the mythical trumpets calling men to crusade. The ringing peal that for the last ten thousand years has sent Man out to war, clutching at his sword.

"But why?" Kingsley was thundering.

"Because," said the Engineer, "we could not work with them. They could not work with one another. We could hardly understand them. Their process of intelligence was so unfathomable, their thought process so twisted, that understanding was almost impossible. How we ever made them understand sufficiently to bring them here, I will never know. Many times we almost despaired. Their minds are so different from ours, so very, very different. Poles apart in thought."

Why, sure, thought Gary, that would be the way one would expect to find it. There was no such thing as parallel physical evolution, why should there be parallel mental evolution?

"Not that their mentality is not as valid as our intelligence," said the Engineer. "Not that they might not have even a greater grasp of science than we. But there could have been no co-ordination, no understanding for us to work together."

"But," said Caroline, "we can understand your thoughts. You can understand ours. And yet we are as far removed from you as they."

The Engineer said nothing.

"And you look like us," said Tommy, quietly. "We are protoplasm and you are metal, but we each have arms and legs . . ."

"It means nothing," said the Engineer. "Absolutely nothing how a thing is made, the shape that one is made in." There was almost an edge of anger in his thoughts.

"Don't you worry, old man," said Herb. "We'll save the universe. I don't know how in hell we'll do it, but we'll save it for you."

"Not for us," the Engineer corrected, "but for those

others. For all life that now exists within the universe. For all life that in time to come may exist within the universe."

"There," said Gary, hardly realizing that he spoke aloud, "is an ideal big enough for any man."

An ideal. Something to fight for. A spur that kept Man going on, striving, fighting his way ahead.

Save the universe for that monstrosity in the glass sphere with its shifting vapors, for the little, wriggling, slug-like things, for the mottled terror with the droopy mouth and the glint of humor in his eyes.

"But how?" asked Tommy. "How are we going to do it?"

Kingsley ruffled at him. "We'll do it," he thundered.

He wheeled on the Engineer. "Do you know what kind of energy would exist within the inter-space?" he asked.

"No," said the Engineer, "I cannot tell you that. Perhaps the Hellhounds. But that's impossible."

"Is there any other place?" asked Gary in a voice cold as steel. "Anyone else who could tell us?"

"Yes," said the Engineer. "There is one other race. I think that they might tell you. But not yet. Not yet. It is too dangerous."

"We don't care," said Herb. "We humans eat up danger."

"Let us try it," said Gary. "Just a couple of us. If something happened, the others would be left to carry on."

"No," said the Engineer, and there was a terrible finality in the single thought.

"Why can't we go out ourselves and find out?" asked Herb. "We could make a little universe just for ourselves. Float right out into this fifth-dimension space and study the energy that we find."

"Splendid," purred Kingsley. "Absolutely splendid. Except there isn't any energy yet. Won't be until the two universes rub and then it will be too late."

"Yes," said Caroline, smiling at Herb, "we have to know before the energy is produced. When the universes rub, it will flood in upon us in such great quantity that we'll be wiped out almost immediately. The first contracting rush of space and time will engulf us. Remember, we're just inside the universal rim."

"I do not entirely understand," said the Engineer. "You spoke of making a universe. Can you make a universe? Bend space and time around a predetermined mass? I am afraid you jest. That would be difficult."

Gary started. Was it possible that Caroline had done something an Engineer thought impossible to do? Standing here, it seemed so simple, so commonplace that space-time could be bent into a hypersphere. Nothing wonderful about it. Just something to be slightly astonished at and argued about. Just a few equations spread upon a sheet of paper.

"Sure we can," bellowed Kingsley. "This little lady has it figured out."

"The little lady," commented Herb, "is a crackajack at figures."

The Engineer reached out his hand to take the sheet of calculations that Kingsley was handing to him. But as he reached out his arm little red lights began to blink throughout the laboratory and in their ears sounded a shrill, high-pitched whine—a whine that held a note of sinister alarm.

"What's that?" yelled Kingsley, dropping the sheet.

The thought of the Engineer came to them as calm as ever, as absolutely devoid of emotion as it had always been.

"The Hellhounds," he said "The Hellhounds are attacking us."

As he spoke, Gary watched the sheet of paper flutter to the floor, a little fluttering sheet that held the key to the riddle of the universe scratched upon it in the black scrawlings of a soft-lead pencil.

The Engineer moved across the laboratory to a panel. His metallic fingers reached out, deftly punched at studs. A wall screen lighted up and on it they saw the bowl of sky above the city. Ships were shooting up and outward, great silver ships that had grim lines of power about them. Up from the roofs they arrowed out into space, squadron after squadron, following a grim trail to the shock of combat. Going out to meet the Hellhounds.

The Engineer made adjustments on the panel and they were looking deeper into space, far out into the darkness where the atmosphere had ended. A tiny speck of silver appeared and rapidly leaped toward them, dissolving into a cloud of ships. Thousands of them.

"The Hellhounds," said the Engineer.

Gary heard Herb suck in his breath, saw Kingsley's hamlike hands clenching and unclenching.

"Stronger than ever," said the Engineer. "Perhaps with new and more deadly weapons, perhaps more efficient screens. I am afraid, so very much afraid, that this means the end of us ... and of the universe."

"How far away are they?" asked Tommy.

"Only a few thousand miles now," said the Engineer. "Our alarm system warns us when they are within ten thousand miles of the surface. That gives us time to get our fleet out into space to meet them."

"Is there anything we can do?" asked Gary.

"We are doing everything we can," said the Engineer.

"But I don't mean you," said Gary. "Is there anything the five of us can do? Any war service we can render you?"

"Not now," said the Engineer. "Perhaps later there will be something. But not now."

He adjusted the screen again and in it they watched the defending ships of the Engineers shooting spaceward, maneuvered into far-flung battle lines—like little dancing motes against the black of space.

In breathless attention they kept their eyes fixed on the screen, saw the gleaming points of light draw closer together, the invaders and the defenders. Then upon the screen they saw dancing flashes that were not reflections from the ships, but something else—knifing flashes that reached out, probed and stabbed and slashed, like a searchlight's beam cuts into the night. A tiny pinpoint of red light flashed momentarily and then went out. Another flamed, like lightning bugs of a summer night, except the flash was red and seemed filled with a terrible violence.

"Those flashes," breathed Caroline. "What are they?"

"Exploding ships," said the Engineer. "Screens break

down and the energy drains out and then an atomic bomb or ray finds its way into them."

"Exploding ships," said Gary. "But whose?"

"How can I tell?" asked the Engineer. "It may be theirs or ours."

Even as he spoke a little ripple of red flashes ran across the screen.

Chapter Ten

HALF the city was in ruins, swept and raked by the stabbing rays that probed down from the upper reaches of the atmosphere, blasted by hydrogen and atomic bombs that shook the very bedrock of the planet and shattered great, sky-high towers of white masonry into drifting dust. Twisted wreckage fell into the city from the battle area, great cruisers reduced to grotesque metal heaps, bent and burned and battered out of all semblance to a ship, scorched and crushed and flattened by the energy unloosed in the height of battle.

"They have new weapons," said the Engineer. "New weapons and better screens. We can hold them off a little longer. How much longer I do not know."

In the laboratory, located in the base of one of the tallest of the skyscrapers in the great white city, the Engineers and the Earthlings had watched the battle for long hours. Had seen the first impact of the fleets, had watched the first dogfight out at the edge of atmosphere, had witnessed the Hellhounds slowly drive the defenders back until the invaders were within effective bombardment distance of the city itself.

"They have a screen stripper," said the Engineer, "that is far more effective than anything we have ever seen. It is taking too much of our ships' energy to hold up their screens under this new weapon."

In the telescopic screen a brilliant blue-white flash filled all the vision-plate as a bomb smashed into one of the few remaining towers. The tower erupted with a flash of blinding light and disappeared, with merely the ragged stump of masonry bearing mute testimony to its once sky-soaring height.

"Isn't there anyone who can help us?" asked Kingsley. "Surely there is someone to whom we might appeal."

"There is no one," said the Engineer. "We are alone. For thousands of light years there are no other great races to be found. For millions of years the Hellhounds and the Engineers have fought, and it has always been those two and just those two alone. Thus it is now. Before, we have driven them off. Many times have we destroyed them almost to the point of annihilation that we might hold their cosmic ambitions under proper check. Now it seems they will be the victors."

"No other race," said Gary, musing, "for thousands of light years."

He stared moodily at the screen, saw a piece of twisted wreckage that had at one time been a ship crash into the stump of broken tower and hang there, like a bloody, smoke-blackened offering tossed on the altar of war.

"But there is," he said. "There is at least one great race very near to us."

"There is?" asked Caroline. "Where?"

"On the other universe," said Gary. "A race that is fully as great, as capable as the Engineers. A race that should be glad to help us in this fight."

"Great suffering snakes," yelped Herb, "why didn't we think of that before?"

"I do not understand," said the Engineer. "I agree they are a great race and very close to us. Much too close, in fact. But they might as well be a billion light years away. They can do us no good. How would you get them here?"

"Yes," rumbled Kingsley, "how would you get them here?"

Gary turned to the Engineer. "You have talked to them," he said. "Have you any idea of what kind of people they might be?"

"A great people," said the Engineer. "Greater than we in certain sciences. They are the ones who notified us of the danger of the approaching universes. They knew they were nearing our universe when we didn't even know there was another universe other than our own. Such very clever people."

"Talk to them again," said Gary. "Give them the information that will enable them to make a miniature universe . . . one of Caroline's hyperspheres."

"But," said the Engineer, "that would do no good."

"It would," said Gary, grimly, "if they could use the laws of space to form a blister on the surface of their universe. If they could go out to the very edge of their space-time frame and create a little bubble of space—a bubble that would pinch off, independent of the parent universe and exist independently in the five-dimension inter-space."

Gary heard the rasp of Kingsley's breath in his helmet phones.

"They could cross to our universe," rumbled the scientist. "They could navigate through the inter-space with complete immunity."

Gary nodded inside his helmet. "Exactly," he said.

"Why, Gary," whispered Caroline, "what a thought!"

"Boy," said Herb, "I can hardly wait to see them Hell-hounds when we sic those fellows on them."

"Maybe," said Tommy, "they won't come."

"I will talk to them," said the Engineer.

He left the room and they followed him through a mighty corridor to another room filled with elaborate machinery.

The Engineer strode to a control panel and worked with dials and studs. Intense blue power surged through long tubes and flashed in dizzy whirls through coils of glass. Tubes boomed into sudden brilliance and the deep hum of power surged into the room.

They could hear the probing fingers of the Engineer's thoughts, thrusting out, calling to those other people in another universe. The power of thought being hurled through the very warp and weave of twisted time and space.

Then came another probing thought, a string of thoughts that were impossible to understand, hazed and blurred and all distorted. But apparently perfectly clear to the Engineer, who stood motionless under the inverted cone of glass that shimmered with blue fire of power.

Two entities talking to one another and the queer, challenging unknown of five-dimensional inter-space separating them!

The power ebbed and the blue fire sank to a glimmer in the tubes.

The Engineer turned around and faced the Earthlings.

"They will come," he said, "but only on one condition."

Suddenly a shiver went through Gary. Condition! That was something he hadn't thought about—that these other things might exact terms, might want concessions, might seek to wring from another universe some measure of profit for a service done.

He had always thought of them as benevolent beings, entities like the Engineers, living a life of service, establishing themselves as guardians of their universe. But that was it. Would they go out of their way to save another universe? Or would they fight only for their own? Was there such a thing as selflessness and universal brotherhood? Or must the universes, in time to come, be forever at one another's throats, as in ancient times nations had torn at one another in savage anger, in more recent times planets had warred for their selfish interests?

"What condition?" asked Kingsley.

"That we or they find out something concerning the nature of the inter-space and of the energy which will be generated when the universes rub," said the Engineer. "They are willing to come and fight for us, but they are not willing to deliberately invite disaster to themselves. No one knows what the inter-space is like. No one knows what laws of science it may hold. There may be laws that are utterly foreign to both our universes, laws that would defy our every bit of knowledge. They are afraid that the budding of a smaller universe from the surface of their own might serve to generate the energy they know will result when two four-dimensional frames draw close to one another."

"Now, wait," said Gary. "There is something I didn't consider when I proposed this thing. It just occurred to me now. When you said the word 'condition,' it came to my mind that they might want concessions or promises. I was wrong, interpreted the thought wrong. But the idea is still there. We don't know what these things in the other universe might be. We don't know what they look like or what their philosophy is or what they can do. If we allowed them to come here, we'd be giving them a key to this universe. Just opening the door for them. They might be all right and they might not. They might take over the universe."

"There's something to that," said Tommy. "We should have thought of it before."

"I do not believe it," said the Engineer. "I have some reason to believe they would not be a menace to us."

"What reason?" rumbled Kingsley.

"They notified us of the danger," said the Engineer.

"They wanted help," said Tommy.

"We have been of little help to them," said the Engineer.

"What difference does it make?" asked Herb. "Unless we can do something about this energy, we're going to be goners, anyhow. And that goes for the other universe as well. If they could save themselves by ruining us, maybe they'd do it, but it's a cinch that if we puff out they go along with us."

"That's right," agreed Kingsley. "It would be to their interest to help us beat off the Hellhounds on the chance that we might find something to save the universes. They wouldn't be very likely to turn on us until somebody had figured out something about this energy."

"And we can't control something we don't understand," said Caroline. "We have to find out what that energy is, what it's like, what form it is apt to take, something about it, so we will know how to handle it."

"How much more time have we to find some way to save us from the big explosion?" asked Gary.

"Very little time," said the Engineer. "Very little time. We are perilously close to the danger point. Shortly the two space-time frames of the two universes will start reacting upon one another, creating the lines of force and stress that will set up the energy fields in the inter-space."

"And you say there is another race that can tell us about this inter-space?"

"One other race I know of," said the Engineer. "There may be others, but I know only of this one. And it is hard to reach. Perhaps impossible to reach."

"Listen," said Gary, "it is our only chance. We might as well fail in reaching them as waiting here for the energy to come and wipe us out. Let a couple of us try. The others may find something else before it is too late. Caroline's hyperspheres might take care of the energy, but we can't be sure. And we have to be sure. The universe depends upon us being sure. We can't just shoot in the dark. We have to know."

"And if we find out," said Herb, "those guys over in the other universe can come over and help us hold the Hellhounds off while we rig up the stuff we have to have."

"I'm afraid," said Kingsley, "we have to take the chance."

"Chance," said the Engineer. "It's a whole lot more than chance. The place I have in mind may not even exist."

"May not even exist?" asked Caroline and there was an edge of terror in her words.

"It is far away," said the Engineer. "Not far in space . . . perhaps even close to us in space. But far away in time."

"In time?" asked Tommy. "Some great civilization of the past?"

"No," said the Engineer. "A civilization of the future. A civilization which may never exist. One that may never come to be."

"How do you know about it, then?" flared Gary.

"I followed its world line," said the Engineer. "And yet not its actual world line, but the world line that was to come. I traced it into the realm of probability. I followed it ahead in time, saw it as it is not yet, as it may never be. I saw the shadow of its probability."

Gary's head reeled. What talk was this? Following of probable world lines. Tracing the course of an empire before it had occurred! Seeing a place that might not ever exist. Talking of sending someone to a place that might never be!

But Caroline was talking now, her cool voice smooth and calm, but with a trace of excitement tinging the tenor of her words.

"You mean you used a geodesic tracer to follow the world line into probability. That you established the fact that in some future time a certain world may exist under such conditions as you saw. That barring unforeseen circumstances it will exist as you saw it, but that you cannot be certain it ever will exist, for the world line you traced could not take into account that factor of accident which might destroy the world or divert it from the path you charted, the path that it logically would have to take."

"That is correct," said the Engineer. "Except for one thing. And that is that the world will exist as I saw it in some measure. For all probabilities must exist to some extent. But its existence might be so tenuous that we could never reach it . . . that for us, in hard, solid fact, it would have no real existence. In other words, we could not set foot upon it. For every real thing there are infinite probabilities, all existing, drawing some shadow of existence from the mere fact that they are probable or have been probable or will be probable. The stress and condition of circumstance selects one of these probabilities, makes it an actuality. But the others have an existence, just the same. An existence, perhaps, that we could not perceive."

"But you did see this shadow of probability?" rumbled Kingsley.

"Yes," said the Engineer, "I saw it very plainly. So plainly that I am tempted to believe it may be an actuality in time to come. But of that I cannot be sure. As I said, it may not exist, may never exist—at least to an extent where we could reach it—where it would have any bearing on our lives."

"There is a chance, though, that we could reach it?" asked Gary.

"There is a chance," said the Engineer.

"Then," said Herb, impatiently, "what are we waiting for?"

"But," said Gary, "if the universe is destroyed, if we should fail and the universe be destroyed, would that probability still be there? Wouldn't the fact that you saw it prove that we will find some way to save the universe?"

"It proves nothing," said the Engineer. "Even were the universe destroyed, the probability would still exist, for the world *could have been*. Destruction of the universe would be a factor of accident which would eliminate actuality and force all lines of probability to remain mere probability."

"You mean," breathed Caroline, "that we could go to a world which exists only as a probable world line and get information there to save the universe—that even after the universe is destroyed, if we fail and it is destroyed, the information which might have saved it still could be found, but too late, of course, to be of any use to us, on that probable world?"

"Yes," said the Engineer, "but there would be no one to find it then. The solution would be there, never used, at a time when it would be too late to use it. It is so hard to explain this thought as it should be explained."

"Maybe it's all right," said Herb, "but I crave action. When do we start for this place that might not be there when we get where we headed for?"

"I will show you," said the Engineer.

They followed him through a maze of laboratory rooms until they came to one which boasted only one piece of equipment, a huge polished bowl set in the floor, blazing with reflected light from the single lamp that shone in the ceiling above it.

The Engineer indicated the bowl.

"Watch," he told them.

He walked to a board on the opposite wall and swiftly set up an equation on a calculating machine. The machine whirred and clicked and chuckled and the Engineer depressed a series of studs in the control board. The inside of the bowl clouded and seemed to take on motion, like a gigantic whirlpool of flowing nothingness. Faster and faster became the impression of motion.

Gary found himself unable to pull his eyes away from

the wonder of the bowl—as if the very motion were hypnotic.

Then the swirl of motion began to take form, misty, tenuous form, as if they were viewing a strange solar system from a vast distance. The solar system faded from view as the vision in the bowl narrowed down to one planet. Other planets flowed out of the picture and the one grew larger and larger, a ball swinging slowly in space.

Then it filled all the bowl and Gary could see seas and cities and mountains and vast deserts. But the mountains were not high, more like weathered hills than mountains, and the seas were shallow. Deserts covered most of the spinning globe and the cities were in ruins.

There was something tantalizingly familiar about that spinning ball, something that struck a chord of memory, something about the solar system—as if he had seen it once before.

And then it struck him like an open hand across his mouth.

"The Earth!" he cried. "That is the Earth!"

"Yes," said the Engineer, "that is your planet, but you see it as it will be many millions of years from now. It is an old, old planet."

"Or as it may never be," whispered Caroline.

"You are right," said the Engineer. "Or as it may never be."

Chapter Eleven

TOMMY EVANS' ship rested on one of the lower roofs of the city, just outside the laboratories level. In a few minutes now it would be lifted and hurled through a warp of space and time that should place it upon the Earth they had seen in the swirling bowl . . . an Earth that was no more than a probability . . . an Earth that wouldn't exist for millions of years if it ever existed.

"Take good care of that ship," Tommy told Gary.

Gary slapped him on the arm.

"I'll bring it back to you," he said.

"We'll be waiting for you," Kingsley rumbled.

"Hell," moaned Herb, "I never get to have any fun. Here you and Caroline are going out there to the Earth and I got to stay behind."

"Listen," said Gary savagely, "there's no use in risking all our lives. Caroline's going because she may be the only one who could understand what the old Earth people can tell us, and I'm going because I play a better hand of poker. I beat you all, fair and square."

"I was a sucker," mourned Herb. "I should have known you'd have an ace in the hole. You always got an ace in the hole."

Tommy grinned.

"I got a lousy hand," he said. "We should have played more than just one hand."

"It was one way of deciding it," said Gary. "We all wanted to go, so we played one hand of poker. We couldn't waste time for more. I won. What more do you want?"

"You always win," Herb complained.

"Just how much chance have you got?" Tommy asked Caroline.

She shrugged.

"It works out on paper," she declared. "When we came here the Engineers had to distort time and space to get us here, but they distorted the two equally. Same amount of distortion for each. But here you have to distort time a whole lot more. Your factors are different. But we have a good chance of getting where we're going."

"If it's there when you get there . . ." Herb began, but Kingsley growled at him and he stopped.

Caroline was talking swiftly to Kingsley.

"The Engineer understands the equation for the hyperspheres," she was saying. "Work with him. Try to set up several of them in our own space and see if it isn't possible to set up at least one outside the universe. Pinch it off the time-space warp and shove it out into the interspace. We may be able to use it later on."

A blast of sound smote them and the solid masonry beneath their feet shivered to the impact of a bomb. For a single second the flashing blaze of atomic fury made the brilliant sunlight seem pale and dim.

"That one was close," said Tommy.

They were used to bombs now.

Gary craned his neck upward and saw the silvery flash of ships far overhead.

"The Engineers can't hold out much longer," Kingsley rumbled. "If we are going to do anything we have to do it pretty soon."

"There is the old space warp again," said Herb. He pointed upward and the others sighted out into space beyond his pointing finger.

There it was . . . the steady wheel of light, the faint spin of space in motion . . . they had seen back on Pluto. The doorway to another world.

"I guess," said Caroline, "that means we have to go." Her voice caught on something that sounded like a sob.

She turned to Kingsley. "If we don't come back," she said, "try the hyperspheres anyhow. Try to absorb the energy in them. You won't have to control it long. Just long enough so the other universe explodes. Then we'll be safe."

She stepped through the air lock and Gary followed her. He turned back and looked at the three of them . . . great, rumbling Kingsley with his huge head thrust forward, staring through his helmet, with his metalshod fists opening and closing; dapper, debonair Tommy Evans, the boy who had dreamed of flying to Alpha Centauri and had come to the edge of the universe instead; Herb, the dumpy little photographer who was eating out his heart because he couldn't go. Through eyes suddenly bleared with emotion, Gary waved at them and they waved back. And then he hurried into the ship, slammed down the lever that swung tight the air-lock valves.

In the control room he took off his helmet and dropped into the pilot's seat. He looked at Caroline. "Good to get the helmet off," he said.

She nodded, lifting her own off her head.

His fingers tapped out a firing pattern. He hesitated for a moment, his thumb poised over the firing lever.

"Listen, Caroline," he asked, "how much chance have we got?"

"We'll get there," she said.

"No," he snapped, "don't tell me that. Tell me the truth. Have we any chance at all?"

Her eyes met his and her mouth sobered into a thin, straight line.

"Yes, some," she said. "Not quite fifty-fifty. There are so many factors of error, so many factors of accident. Mathematics can't foresee them, can't take care of them, and mathematics are the only signposts that we have."

He laughed harshly.

"We're shooting at a target, don't you see?" she said. "A target millions of light-years away, and millions of years away as well, and you have to have a different set of co-ordinates for both the time and distance. The same set won't do for both. It's difficult."

He looked at her soberly. She said it was difficult. He could only faintly imagine how difficult it might be. Only someone who was a master at the mathematics of both time and space could even faintly understand—someone, say, who had thought for forty lifetimes.

"And even if we do hit the place," he said, "it may not be there."

Savagely he plunged his thumb against the lever. The rockets thundered and the ship was arcing up. Another pattern and another. They were plunging upward now under the full thrust of rocket power and still the ruined city was all around them, cragged, broken towers shattered by the blasting of atomic energy.

The soft swirl of light that marked the opening of the time-space tunnel lay between and beyond two blasted towers. Gary fired a short, corrective pattern to line the nose of the ship between the towers and then depressed a stud and fired a blast that drove them straight between the towers, up and over the city, straight for the whirl of light.

The ship arrowed swiftly up. The directional crosshairs lined squarely upon the hub of spinning light.

"We're almost there," he said, his breath whistling between his teeth. "We'll know in just a minute."

The cold wind out of space was blowing on his face again; the short hairs on his neck were trying to rise into a ruff. The old challenge of the unknown. The old glory of crusading.

He snapped a look at Caroline. She was staring out of the vision plate, staring straight ahead, watching the rim of the wheel spin out until only the blackness of the hub remained.

She turned to him. "Oh, Gary!" she cried, and then the ship plunged into the hub and blackness as thick and heavy and as stifling as the ink of utter space flooded into the ship and seemed to dim the very radium lamps that burned within the room.

He heard her voice coming out of the blackness that engulfed them. "Gary, I'm afraid!"

Then the black was gone and the ship rode in space again—in a star-sprinkled space that had, curiously, a warm and friendly look after the blackness of the tunnel.

"There it is!" Caroline cried, and Gary expelled his breath in a sigh of relief.

Below them swam a planet, a planet such as they had seen in the spinning bowl back in the city of the Engineers. A planet that was spotted with mighty mountains weathered down to meek and somber hills, a planet with shallow seas and a thinning atmosphere.

"The Earth," said Gary, looking at it.

Yes, the Earth. The birthplace of the human race, now an old and senile planet tottering to its doom, a planet that had outlived its usefulness. A planet that had mothered a great race of people—a race that always strove to reach what was just beyond, always reaching out to the not-as-yet, that met each challenge with a battle cry. A crusading people.

"It's really there," said Caroline. "It's real."

Gary glanced swiftly at the instruments. They were only a matter of five hundred miles above the surface and as yet there was no indication of atmosphere. Slowly the ship was dropping toward the planet, but still there was no sign of anything but space.

He whistled softly. Even the slightest presence of gases

would be registered on the dials and so far the needles hadn't even flickered.

Earth must be old! Her atmosphere was swiftly being stripped from her to leave her bare bones naked to the cold of space. Space, cold and malignant, was creeping in on mankind's cradle.

He struck the first sign of atmosphere at slightly under two hundred miles.

The surface of the planet was lighted by a Sun which must have lost much of its energy, for the light seemed feeble compared to the way Gary remembered it. The Sun, behind them, was shielded from their vision.

Swiftly they dropped, closer and closer to the surface. Eagerly they scanned the land beneath them for some sign of cities, but they saw only one and that, the telescope revealed, was in utter ruins. Drifting sands were closing over its shattered columns and once mighty walls.

"It must have been a great city in its day," said Caroline softly. "I wonder what has happened to the people."

"Died off," said Gary, "or left for some other planet, maybe for some other sun."

The telescopic screen mirrored scene after scene of desolation. Vast deserts with shifting dunes and mile after mile of nothing but shimmering sand, without a trace of vegetation. Worn-down hills with boulder-strewn slopes and wind-twisted trees and shrubs making their last stand against the encroachment of a hostile environment.

Gary turned the ship toward the night side of the planet, and it was then they saw the Moon. Vast, filling almost a twelfth of the sky, it loomed over the horizon, a monstrous orange ball in full phase.

"How pretty!" gasped Caroline.

"Pretty and dangerous," said Gary.

It must be approaching Roche's limit, he thought. Falling out of the sky, year after year it had drawn closer to the Earth. When it reached a certain limit, it would be disrupted, torn to bits by the stresses of gravitation hauling and tugging at it. It would shatter into tiny fragments and those fragments would take up independent orbits around old Earth, giving her in miniature the rings of Saturn. But the same forces which would tear the Moon to bits, would shake up the Earth, giving rise to volcanic action, world-shattering earthquakes, monstrous tidal waves. Mountains would be leveled, new continents raised. Earth's face would be changed once again, as it probably had been changed many times before. As it had been changed since early Man had known it, for search as he might, Gary could find no single recognizable feature, not a single sea or continent that seemed familiar.

He reflected on the changes that must have come to pass. The Earth must have slowed down. Probably a night now was almost a month long, and a day equally as long. Long scorching days and endless frigid nights. Century after century, with the moon tides braking the Earth's motion, with the addition of mass due to falling meteors, Earth had lost her energy. Increase of mass and loss of energy had slowed her spin, had shoved her farther and farther away from the Sun, pushing her out and into the frigidness of space. And now she was losing her atmosphere. Her gravity was weakening and the precious gases were slowly being stripped from her. Rock weathering also would have absorbed some of the oxygen.

"Look!" cried Caroline.

Aroused from his daydreaming, Gary saw a city straight ahead, looming on the horizon, a great city a-gleam with shining metal.

"The Engineer said we would find people here," Caroline whispered. "That must be where we'll find them."

The city was falling into ruin. Much of it, undoubtedly, already had been covered by the creeping desert that crawled toward it from every direction. Some of the buildings were falling apart, with great gaping holes staring like empty, hopeless eyes. But part of it, at least, was standing, and that part gave a breath-taking hint to the sort of city it had been when it soared in full pride of strength at its very prime.

Smoothly Gary brought the ship down toward the city, down toward a level patch of desert in front of the largest building yet standing. And the building, he saw, was a beauteous thing that almost defied description, a poem in grace and rhythm, seemingly too fragile for this weird and bitter world.

The ship plowed along the sand and stopped.

Gary rose from the pilot's seat and reached for his helmet. "We're here," he announced.

"I didn't think we'd make it," Caroline confessed. "We took such an awful chance."

"But we did," he said gruffly. "And we have a job to do."

He set his helmet on his head and clamped it down. "I have a hunch we'll need these things," he said.

She put on her helmet and together they went out of the air lock.

Wind keened thinly over the empty deserts and the ruins, kicked up little puffs of sand that raced and danced weird rigadoons across the dunes and past the ship, up to the very doors of the shiny building that confronted them.

A slinking shape slunk across a dune and streaked swiftly for the shelter of a pile of fallen masonry—a little furtive shape that might have been a skulking dog or something else, almost anything at all.

A sense of desolation smote Gary and he felt an alien fear gripping at his soul.

He shivered. This wasn't the way a man should feel on his own home planet. This wasn't the way a man should feel on coming home from the very edge of everything.

But it wasn't the edge of everything, he reminded himself. It was just the edge of the universe. For the universe wasn't everything. Beyond it, stretching for uncountable, mind-shattering distances, were other universes. The universe was just a tiny unit of the whole, perhaps as tiny a unit of the whole as the Earth was a tiny unit of its universe. A grain of sand upon the beach, he thought—less than a grain of sand upon the beach.

And this might not be Earth, of course. It might be just the shadow of the Earth—a probability that gained strength and substance and a semblance of being because it missed being an actuality by a mere hair's-breadth.

His mind whirled at the thought of it, at the astounding vista of possibilities that the thought brought up, the infinite number of possibilities that existed as shadows, each with a queer shadow existence of its very own, things that just missed being realities. Disappointed ghosts, he thought, wailing their way through the eternity of nonexistence.

Caroline was close beside him. Her voice came to him through the helmet phones, a tiny voice. "Gary, everything is so strange."

"Yes," he said. "Strange."

Cautiously they walked forward, toward the gaping door of the great metal building from whose turrets and spires and froth of superstructure the moonbeams splintered in a cold glitter of faery beauty.

Sand crunched and grated underfoot. The wind made shrill, keening noises and they could see the frozen frost crystals in the sand, moisture locked in the grip of deadly cold.

They reached the doorway and peered inside. The interior was dark and Gary unhooked the radium lamp from his belt. The lamp cut a broad beam of light down the mighty, high-arched hallway that led straight from the door toward the center of the building.

Gary caught his breath, seized with a nameless fear, the fear of the dark and the unfamiliar, of the ghostly and the ancient.

"We might as well go in," he said, fighting down the fear.

Their footsteps echoed and re-echoed in the darkness as the metal of their boots rang against the cold paving blocks.

Gary felt the weight of centuries pressing down upon him—the eyes of many nations and of many people watching furtively, jealous to guard old tradition from the invasion of an alien mind. For he and Caroline, he sensed, were aliens here, aliens in time if not in blood. He sensed it in the very architecture of the place, in the atmosphere of the long and silent hall, in the quiet that brooded on this dead or dying planet.

Suddenly they left the hallway and were striding into what seemed a vast chamber. Gary snapped the lamp to full power and explored the place. It was filled with furniture. Solid blocks of seat faced a rostrum, and all about the wall ran ornate benches.

At one time, now long gone, it might have been a council hall, a meeting place of the people to decide great issues. In this room, he told himself, history might have been written, the course of cosmic empire might have been shaped and the fate of stars decided.

But now there was no sign of life, just a brooding silence that seemed to whisper in a tongueless language of days and faces and problems long since wiped out by the march of years.

He looked about and shivered.

"I don't like this place," said Caroline.

A light suddenly flared and blazed as a door opened and thought-fingers reached out to them, thoughts that were kindly and definitely human:

"Do you seek someone here?"

Chapter Twelve

STARTLED, they swung around. A stooped old man stood in a tiny doorway that opened from the hall—an old man who, while he was human, seemed not quite human. His head was large and his chest bulged out grotesquely. He stood on trembly pipestem legs and his arms were alarmingly long and skinny.

A long white beard swept over his chest, but his great domed head was innocent of even a single hair. Across the space that separated them, Gary felt the force of piercing eyes that stared out from under shaggy eyebrows.

"We're looking for someone," said Gary, "to give us information."

"Come in," shrieked the thought of the old man. "Come in. Do you want me to catch my death of cold holding the door open for you?"

Gary grasped Caroline by the hand. "Come on," he said.

At a trot, they crossed the room, ducked through the door. They heard the door slam behind them and turned to look at the old man.

He stared back at them. "You are human beings," said his thoughts. "People of my own race. But from long ago."

"That's right," said Gary. "From many millions of years ago."

They sensed something that almost approached disbelief in the old man's thoughts.

"And you seek me?"

"We seek someone," said Gary. "Someone who may tell us something that may save the universe."

"Then it must be me," said the old man, "because I'm the only one left."

"The only one left!" cried Gary. "The last man?"

"That's right," said the old man, and he seemed almost cheerful about it. "There were others but they died. All men's life spans must sometime come to an end."

"But there are others," persisted Gary. "You can't be the last man left alive."

"There were others," said the old one, "but they left. They went to a far star. To a place prepared for them."

A coldness gripped Gary's heart.

"You mean they died?"

The old man's thoughts were querulous and impatient. "No, they did not die. They went to a better place. To a place that has been prepared for them for many years. A place where they could not go until they were ready."

"But you?" asked Gary.

"I stayed because I wanted to," said the old man. "Myself and a few others. We could not forsake Earth. We elected to stay. Of those who stayed all the others have died and I am left alone."

Gary glanced around the room. It was tiny, but comfortable. A bed, a table, a few chairs, other furniture he did not recognize.

"You like my place?" asked the old man.

"Very much," said Gary.

"Perhaps," said the old man, "you would like to take off your helmets. It's warm in here and I keep the atmosphere a little denser than it is outside. Not necessary that I do so, of course, but it is more comfortable. The atmosphere is getting pretty thin and hard to breathe."

They unfastened their helmets and lifted them off. The air was sharp and tangy, the room was warm.

"That's better," said Caroline.

"Chairs?" asked the old man, pointing out a couple.

They sat and he lowered his old body into another.

"Well, well," he said, and his thoughts had a grandfatherly touch about them, "humans of an earlier age. Splendid physical specimen, the two of you. And fairly barbaric still—but the stuff is in you. You use your mouths to talk with and man hasn't talked with other than his thoughts for thousands and thousands of years. That in itself would set you pretty far back."

"Pretty far is right," said Gary. "We are the first humans who ever left the solar system."

"That is far," said the old man. "Far, far . . ."

His sharp eyes watched them closely. "You must have an interesting story," he suggested.

"We have," said Caroline and swiftly they told it to him, excitedly, first one and then the other talking, adding in details, explaining situations, laying before him the problems which they faced.

He listened intently, snapping questions now and then, his bright old eyes shining with the love of adventure, the wrinkles in his face taking on a kind benevolence as if they might be children, home from the first day of school, telling of all the new wonders they had met.

"So you came to me," he said. "You came trundling down a crazy timepath to seek me out. So that I could tell you the things you need to know."

Caroline nodded. "You can tell us, can't you?" she asked. "It means so much to us—so much to everyone."

"I wouldn't worry," said the old man. "If the universe had come to an end, I wouldn't be here. You couldn't have come to me."

"But maybe you aren't real," said Caroline. "Maybe you are just a shadow. A probability . . ."

The oldster nodded and combed his beard with gnarled fingers. The breath wheezed in his mighty chest.

"You are right," he agreed. "I may be only a shadow. This world of mine may be no more than a shadow-world. I sometimes wonder if there is any reality at all—if there is anything but thought. Whether it may not be that some gigantic intelligence has dreamed all these things we see and believe in and accept as real . . . if the giant intelligence may not have set mighty dream stages and peopled them with actors of his imagination. I wonder at times if all the universes may be nothing more than a shadow show. A company of shadowy actors moving on a shadow stage."

"But you can tell us," pleaded Caroline. "You will tell us."

His old eyes twinkled. "I will tell you, yes, and gladly. Your fifth dimension is eternity. It is everything and nothing . . . all rolled into one. It is a place where nothing has ever happened and yet, in a sense, where everything has happened. It is the beginning and the end of all things. In it there is no such thing as space or time or any other phenomena which we attribute to the four-dimensional continuum."

"I can't understand," said Caroline, lines of puzzlement twisting her face. "It seems so hopeless, so entirely hopeless. Can it be explained by mathematics?"

"Yes," said the old man, "but I'm afraid you wouldn't understand. The mathematics necessary to explain it weren't evolved until just a few thousand years ago."

He stroked the beard down smoothly over his pouter-pigeon chest.

"I do not wish to make you feel badly," he declared, "but I can't see how you would have the intelligence to grasp it. After all, you are a people from an earlier age, an almost barbaric age."

"Try her," growled Gary.

"All right," said the old man, but there was a patronizing tone to his thoughts.

Gary gained a confused impression of horrific equations, of bracketed symbols that built themselves into a tangled and utterly confused structure of meaning—a meaning that seemed so vast and all-inclusive that his mind instinctively shuddered away from it.

Then the thoughts were gone and Gary's mind was spinning with them, with the vital forcefulness that he had guessed and glimpsed behind the symbolic structure that had been in the mathematics.

He looked at Caroline and saw that she was puzzled. But suddenly a look of awe spread over her face.

"Why," she said, and hesitated slightly, ". . . . why, the equations cancel, represent both everything and nothing, both zero and the ultimate in everything imaginable."

Gary caught a sense of surprise and confusion that flashed through the mind of their host.

"You understand," said the faltering thought. "You grasp the meaning perfectly."

"Didn't I tell you," said Gary. "Of course, she understands."

Caroline was talking, almost as if she were talking to herself, talking her thoughts aloud. "That means the energy would be timeless. It would have no time factor, and since time is a factor in power, its power would be almost infinite. There'd be no stopping it, once it started."

"You are right," said the old man. "It would be raw, created energy from a region where four-dimensional laws are no longer vaild. It would be timeless and formless."

"Formless," said Caroline. "Of course, it would be formless. It wouldn't be light, or heat, or matter, or motion, or any other form of energy such as we know. But it could be anything. It would be waiting to become something. It could crystallize into anything."

"Good Lord," said Gary, "how could you handle stuff like that? Your hyperspheres wouldn't handle it. It could mold space itself. It could annihilate time."

Caroline looked at him soberly.

"If I could create a fifth-dimensional trap," she said, "if I could trap it in the framework of the medium from which it came. Don't you see that such a framework would attract it, would gather it in and hold it. Like a battery holds energy. Like water seeking its own level and coming to rest."

"Sure," agreed Gary, "if you could create a fifth-dimensional trap. But you can't. It's eternity. The dimension of eternity. You can't go fooling around with eternity."

"Yes, she can," said the old man.

The two of them stared at him, not believing.

"Listen closely," said the oldster. "By rotating a circle through three dimensions you create a sphere. Rotate the sphere through four dimensions and you have a hypersphere. You already have created this. You have bent time and space around a mass to create a hypersphere, a miniature universe. Now all you have to do is rotate the hypersphere through five-dimensional space."

"But you'd have to be in five-dimensional space to do that," objected Gary.

"No, you wouldn't," contended the old man. "Scattered throughout three-dimensional space are ether eddies and time faults and space traps—call them anything you like. They are a common phenomena and they're nothing more, when you come right down to it, than isolated bits of four-dimensional space scattered around through three-dimensional space. The same thing would apply to a fifth dimension in the fourth dimension."

"But how," asked Caroline, "would one go about it? How would one rotate a hypersphere through the fifth dimension?"

Again Gary had that sense of confusion as the thoughts of the ancient one swept over him, thoughts that translated themselves into symbols and equations and brackets of mathematics that it seemed impossible any man could know.

"Gary," gasped Caroline, "have you a pencil and some paper?"

Gary fumbled in his pocket and found an old envelope and a stub of pencil. He handed them to her.

"Please repeat that very slowly," she said, smiling at the old man.

Gary watched in amazement as Caroline, slowly and carefully, jotted down the formulas, equations, symbols—carefully checking and going over them, checking and rechecking so there could be no mistake.

"It will take power," she said. "Tremendous power. I wonder if the Engineers can supply it."

"They have magnetic power," said Gary. "They ought to be able to give you all you need."

The old man's eyes were twinkling. "I am remembering the Hellhounds," he said. "The ones who would have the universe destroyed. I cannot seem to like them. It seems to me that something should be done about them."

"But what?" asked Gary. "They seem to be all powerful. By the time we get back they may have battered the city into a mass of ruins."

The oldster nodded almost sleepily, but his eyes were glowing.

"We have had ones like that in our history," he said. "Ones who overrode the nations and imposed their will, standing in the way of progress. But always someone found something that would break them. Someone found a greater weapon or a greater strength and they went their way. Their names and works were dust and they were forgotten and the civilization that they sought to mold to their own selfish ends went on as if they had never been."

"But I don't see . . ." began Gary, and then suddenly he did—as clearly as light. He smote his knee and yelled his enthusiasm.

"Of course," he cried. "We have a weapon. A weapon that could wipe them out. The fifth-dimensional energy!"

"Certainly you have," said the old man.

"That would be barbarous," protested Caroline.

"Barbarous!" shouted Gary. "Isn't it barbarous to want to see the universe destroyed so the Hellhounds can go back to the beginning and take it over, control it, dominate it, take over galaxy after galaxy as a new universe is born? Shape it to their needs and desires. Hold in thrall every bit of life that develops on every cooling planet. Become the masters of the universe."

"We must hurry, then," said Caroline. "We must get back. Minutes count. We still may be able to save the Engineers and the universe, wipe out the Hellhounds."

She rose impatiently to her feet.

The old man protested. "You would go so soon?" he asked. "You would not stay and eat with me? Or tell me more about this place at the edge of the universe? Or let me tell you strange things that I know you would be glad to hear?"

Gary hesitated. "Maybe we could stay a while," he suggested.

"No," said Caroline. "We must go."

"Listen," said Gary to the old man, "why don't you come along with us? We'd be glad to have you. We could use you in the fight. There are things that you could tell us that would help."

The old man shook his head. "I cannot go," he said. "For, you see, you are right. I may be only a shadow. A very substantial shadow, perhaps, but still just a shadow of probability. You can come to me, but I can't go back with you. If I left this planet I might puff into nothingness, revert to the non-existence of the thing that never was."

He hesitated. "But there's something," he said, "that makes me suspect I am not a shadow . . . that this is actuality, that the Earth will follow the course history tells me it has followed."

"What is that?" asked Gary.

"It is a thing," the old man said, "that I cannot tell you."

"Perhaps we can come back and see you again," said Caroline. "After all this trouble is over."

"No, my child," he said. "You will never come, for ours are lives that never should have met. You represent the beginning and I represent the end. And I am proud that the Earth's last man could have been of service to one of the beginners."

They fastened down their helmets and walked toward the door.

"I will walk with you to your ship," said the old man. "I do not walk a great deal now, for the cold and the thin air bother me. I must be getting old."

Their feet whispered through the sand and the wind keened above the desert, a shrill-voiced wind that played an eternal overture for the stage of desolation old Earth had become.

"I live with ghosts," said the old man as they walked toward the ship. "Ghosts of men and events and great ideals that built a mighty race.

"Probably you wonder that I resemble a man so much. Perhaps you thought that men, in time to come, would evolve into specialized monstrosities—great, massive brains that had lost the power of locomotion, or bundles of emotional reactions, unstable as the very wind, or foolish philosophers, or, worse yet, drab realists. But we became none of these things. We kept our balance. We kept our feet on the ground when dreams filled our heads."

They reached the ship and stood before the opened outer valve.

The old man waved a hand toward the mighty metal building.

"The proudest city Man ever built," he said. "A city whose fame spread to the far stars, to distant galaxies. A city that travelers told about in bated whispers. A place to which came the commerce of many solar systems, ships from across far inter-galactic space. But now it is crumbling into dust and ruin. Soon the desert will claim it and the wind will sing a death dirge for it and little, furry animals will burrow in its bones."

He turned to them and Gary saw a half-mystic light shining in his eyes.

"Thus it is with cities," he said, "but Man is different. Man marches on and on. He outgrows cities and builds others. He outgrows planets. He is creating a heritage, a mighty heritage that in time will make him the master of the universe.

"But there will be interludes of defeat. Times when it seems that all is lost—that Man will slip again to the primal savagery and ignorance. Times when the way seems too hard and the price too great to pay. But always there will be bugles in the sky and a challenge on the horizon and the bright beckoning of ideals far away. And Man will go ahead, to greater triumphs, always pushing back the frontiers, always moving up and outward."

The old man turned around and headed back toward the doorway in the building. He went without a word of farewell and his sandaled feet left a tiny, ragged trail across the shifting sand.

Chapter Thirteen

THE black tunnel of the space-time wheel ended and the ship was in normal space again.

Normal, but not right.

Gary, hunched over the controls, heard Caroline's quick gasp of surprise.

"There's something wrong!" she cried.

There was a world, but it was not the planet of the Engineers. No great city grew upon it from horizon to horizon. Instead of three blue suns, there was one and it was very large and red, a dull brick red, and its rays were so feeble that one could stare straight into it and at the edges it seemed that one could see straight through the fringe of gases.

There was no Hellhounds fleet, no flashing ships of the defender . . . no war.

There was peace upon this world . . . a quiet and deadly peace. The peace, thought Gary, of the neverwas, the peace of all-is-over.

It was a flat splotched world with a leprous look about it, not gray, but colored as a child with water paints might color a paint book page when he was tired and all the need of accuracy and art were things to be forgotten.

Something happened, Gary told himself. And he felt the chill of fear in his veins.

Something happened and here we are—in what strange corner of the universe?

"Something went wrong," Caroline said again. "Some inherent weakness in the co-ordinates, some streak of instability in the mathematics themselves, perhaps."

"More likely," Gary told her, "the fault lies in the human brain—or in the brain of the Engineer. No man, no being, can see far enough ahead, think so clearly that he will foresee each eventuality. And even if he did, he might be inclined to let some small factor slip by with no other thought than that it was so small it could do no harm."

Caroline nodded at him. "The mistakes creep in so easy," she admitted. "Like mice . . . mice running in the mind."

"We can turn around and go back," said Gary, but even as he said it he knew that it was no good. For if the tunnel of distorted time-space through which they had come was jiggered out of position at this end, it would be out of focus at the other end as well.

"But we can't," said Caroline.

"I know we can't," said Gary. "I spoke too quickly. Without thinking."

"We can't even try," said Caroline. "The wheel is gone."

He saw that she was right. The wheel of light was no longer in the sky. It had snuffed out and they were here alone.

Here? he asked. And where was here?

There was a simple answer. They simply did not know. At the moment, there was no way of telling.

"Lost," said Caroline. "Like the babes in the woods. The robins came, you remember, and covered them with leaves."

The ship was gliding down toward the planet and Gary swung around to the controls again.

"We'll look it over," he said.

"There may be someone there," said Caroline.

Someone, Gary thought, was not quite the word. Something would be more like it. Some thing.

The planet was flat, a world without mountains, without rivers, without seas. There were great green bogs instead of seas and flat arid plains with splotches of color that might be vegetation or might be no more than the outcropping of different geological strata.

The ship took up its descent spiral and Gary and Caroline hung close above the visor, watching for some sign of habitation, for some hint of life. A road, perhaps. Or a building. Or a vehicle moving on the ground or in the air. But there was nothing.

Finally Gary shook his head. "There's nothing here," he said. "We might as well go down. One place on this planet is as good as any other."

They landed on a flat expanse of sand between the shore of one of the green bogs and the edge of a patch of splotched vegetation, for by now it was apparent that the color spots on the planet's surface were vegetation of a sort.

"Toadstools," said Caroline, looking out the vision plate. "Toadstools and that other kind of funny stuff, like asparagus spears, only it's not asparagus."

"Like something out of a goblin book," said Gary.

Like something that you thought about when you were

a kid and couldn't go to sleep after grandmother had read you some story about a shivery place and you had pulled the covers up over your head and listened for the footsteps to start coming through the dark.

They made the tests and the planet was livable without their suits—slightly high in oxygen, a little colder and a slighter gravity than Earth, but livable.

"Let's go out," said Gary, gruffly, "and have a look around."

"Gary, you sound as if you might be scared."

"I am," he admitted. "Pink with purple spots."

The silence smote them as they stepped outside the ship. An awesome and abiding silence that was louder than a shattering sound.

There was no sound of wind, and no sound of water. No song of birds. No grass to rustle.

The great red sun hung in the sky above them and their shadows were soft and fuzzy on the sand, the faint, fugitive shadows of a cloudy day.

On one hand lay the stagnant pools of water and the hummocks of slimy vegetation that formed the bog and on the other stretched the forest of giant mushrooms, towering to the height of an average man.

"You'd expect to see a goblin," Caroline said, and she shivered as she said it.

All at once the goblin was there.

He stood underneath one of the toadstools and he was looking at them. When he saw that they had seen him, he lowered one eyelid in a ponderous and exaggerated wink and his slobbering mouth twisted into a grimace that might have been a smile. Its skin was mottled and its eyes were narrow, slitted eyes and even as they watched, an exudation of slimy substance welled out of one of the gland-like openings which pitted its face and ran down its cheek and dripped onto its chest.

"Good Lord!" said Gary. "I know that fellow!"

The goblin leaped into the air and cracked its heels together and gobbled like an excited turkey.

"He's the one that was there the day the Engineers held the conference," said Gary. "You remember, when they got all the aliens together—all those that had come through space to the city of the Engineers. It was him—or one just like him. He sat opposite me and he winked at me, just like he did now, and I thought that . . ."

"There's another one," said Caroline.

The second one was perched on top of one of the mushrooms, with his splayed feet swinging over the edge.

Then there was a third one peeping from behind a stem and still another one, sitting on the ground and leaning against a stem. All of them were watching and all of them were grinning, but the grins were enough to strike terror and revulsion into one's soul.

Caroline and Gary retreated backward to the ship, step by slow step until they stood with their backs against it.

Now there was sound, the soft padding of feet coming through the toadstool forest, the clucking noises that the goblins made.

"Let's go away," said Caroline. "Let's get in the ship and go."

"Wait," counseled Gary. "Let us wait a while. We can always go. These things are intelligent. They have to be, since they were among the ones the Engineers called in."

He stepped out from the ship two slow paces and called.

"Hello," he called.

They stopped their clucking and their running and stood and looked at him out of slitted eyes.

"We are friends," said Gary. They didn't move a muscle.

Gary held up his empty hands, palms outward in the human gesture of peace.

"We are friends," he said.

The silence was on the world again—the dreadful, empty silence. The goblins were gone.

Slowly Gary came back to the ship.

"It doesn't work," he said. "I had no reason to believe it would."

"All things," said Caroline, "would not necessarily communicate by sound. That's just one way of making yourself understood. There would be many other ways. These things make sounds. but that doesn't mean they would have to talk with sound. They may have no auditory apparatus. They may not even know that they make sounds, might not know what sound is."

"They're back again," said Gary. "You try this time. Try thinking at them. Pick out one of them and concentrate on him."

A minute passed, a minute of utter silence.

"It's funny," said Caroline. "I couldn't reach them at all. There wasn't even a flicker of response. But I had the feeling that they knew and that they rejected what I tried to tell them. They closed their minds and would not listen."

"They don't talk," said Gary. "And they either can't or won't telepath. What's next?"

"Sign language," Caroline said. "Pictures after that. Pantomime."

But it did no good. The goblins watched with interest when Gary tried sign language. They crept close to watch as he drew diagrams in the sandy soil. And they squealed and chortled when he tried pantomime. But that they understood any of it they gave not a single sign.

Gary came back to the ship.

"They're intelligent," he said. "They have to be, otherwise how would they ever have been brought to the rim of the universe by the Engineers. Something like that takes understanding, a mechanical aptitude, a penchant for higher mathematics."

He gestured in disgust. "And yet," he said, "they do not understand even the most elementary symbolism."

"These ones may not be trained," said Caroline. "There may be others here who are. There may be an elite, an intelligentsia. These may be the peasants and the serfs."

Gary said wearily: "Let's get out of here. Make a circuit or two of the planet. Watch closely for some sign of development, some evidence of culture."

Caroline nodded. "We could have missed it before."

They went into the ship and closed the port behind them. Through the vision plates they saw the goblins, a large crowd of them by now, lined up at the edge of the mushroom forest, staring at the ship.

Gary lowered himself into the pilot's chair, reached out for the warming knob and twisted it over. Nothing happened. He twisted it back and turned it on again. Silence swam within the ship—no sound of warming jets.

Lord, thought Gary, what a place to get stuck.

Outside the ship, equipped with a kit of tools, he crawled into the take-off tubes, took off the plates that housed the warming assembly and pried into their innards.

An hour later he had finished. He crawled out, grimed and smudged with carbon.

"Nothing wrong," he told Caroline. "No reason why they shouldn't work."

He tried again and they didn't work.

He checked the feed line and the wiring. He ripped off the control panel and went over it, wire by wire, relay by relay, tube by tube. There was nothing wrong.

But still it wouldn't work.

"The goblins," Caroline guessed.

He agreed. "It must be the goblins. There is nothing else to think."

But how, he asked himself, could such simple-minded things turn an almost foolproof, letter-perfect spaceship into a heap of junk?

Chapter Fourteen

THE next morning the Hellhounds came, a small ship quartering down out of the dawn light of the great red sun. It came down on a long smooth slant and landed not more than half a mile away, plowing a swath through the mushroom forest as it grounded. There was no mistaking its identity, for its lines were distinctive and the insignia upon its bow was the insignia that both Caroline and Gary had seen many times on the ships that screamed down to lay bombs upon the mighty city of the Engineers.

"And us," said Gary, "with nothing but hand guns in the locker and a ship that we can't lift."

He saw the stricken look on Caroline's face and tried to make amends. "Maybe they won't know who we are," he said. "Maybe they . . ."

"Don't let's fool ourselves," Caroline told him. "They know who we are, all right. More than likely we're the reason that they're here. Maybe they . . ."

She hesitated and Gary asked, "Maybe they what?"

"I was thinking," she said, "that they might have twisted the tunnel. The mathematics might have been all right. Somebody might have brought us here. It might have been the Hellhounds who trapped us here, knowing what we had, knowing the knowledge that we carried. They might have brought us here and now they've come to finish up the job."

"They were not the ones who brought you here," said a voice out of nowhere. "You were brought here but they were not the ones who brought you. They were brought themselves."

Gary whirled around. "Who said that?" he shouted.

"You cannot find me," said the voice, still talking out of nowhere. "Don't waste your time in trying to find me. I brought you here and I brought the others here and only the one of you may leave . . . the humans or the Hellhounds."

"I don't understand," said Gary. "You are mad . . ."

"You are enemies, you and the Hellhounds," said the voice. "You are equal in number and in strength of arms. There are two of you and there are two of them. You have small weapons only and so have they. It will be a fair encounter."

Fantastic, thought Gary. A situation jerked raw from a latter-day Alice in Wonderland. A nightmare twisted out of the strange and grotesque alienness of this splotched planet. A planet filed with goblins and with nightmares— a fairyland turned sour.

"You want us to fight?" he asked. "Fight the Hellhounds? A sort of—well, you might call it a duel?"

"That is exactly it," the voice told him.

"But what good will it do?"

"You are enemies, aren't you, human?"

"Why, yes, we are," said Gary, "but anything that we do here won't affect the war one way or the other."

"You will fight," said the voice. "You are two and they are two and. . . ."

"But one of us is a woman," protested Gary. "Female humans do not engage in duels."

The voice did not answer, but Gary sensed frustration

in a mind—perhaps a presence rather than a mind—that was near to them.

He pressed his advantage. "You say that our arms are equal, that they have small arms only and so have we. But you can't be sure that the arms are equal. Their arms, even if they are no bigger than ours, may be more powerful. Size is not a measure for power. Or their arms may be equal, but the Hellhounds may be better versed in their use."

"They are small weapons," said the voice. "They are..."

"You want this to be a fair fight, don't you?"

"Why, yes," said the voice. "Yes, of course, I do. That is the purpose of it, that everything be even, so that in all fairness the two species may test their true and proper fitness for survival."

"But, you see," said Gary, "you can't be sure it's even. You never can be sure."

"Yes, I can," the voice told him and there was an insane ring of triumph in it. "I can make sure that it will be even. You will fight without weapons. None of you will have weapons. Just bare hands and teeth or whatever else you may have."

"Without..."

"That's it. Neither of you will have weapons."

"But they have guns," said Gary.

"Their guns won't work," the voice said. "And yours won't either. Your ship won't work and your guns won't work and you will have to fight."

Terrible laughter came from the voice, a gleeful laughter that verged on hysteria. Then the laughter ceased and they knew that they were alone, that the mind—or the presence—with the voice had withdrawn from them, that it had gone elsewhere. But that it still was watching.

"Gary," Caroline said softly.

"Yes," said Gary.

"That voice was insane," she said. "You caught it, didn't you. The overtones in it."

He nodded. "Delusion of grandeur. Playing at God. And the worst of it is, he can make it stick. We've stumbled into his yard. There isn't a thing we can do about it."

Across the mushroom forest, the entrance port of the Hellhound ship was swinging open. From it came two beings, tall and waddling things that glimmered in the feeble light of the great red sun.

"Reptilian," said Caroline and there was more disgust than horror in her voice.

The Hellhounds stepped down from the ship and stood uncertainly, their snouted faces turning toward the Earth ship, then swinging from side to side to take in the country.

"Caroline," said Gary, "I'll stay here and watch. You go in and get the guns. They are in the locker."

"They won't work," said Caroline.

"I want to be sure," Gary told her.

He heard her turn from his side and go, climbing up the ladder into the entrance lock.

The Hellhounds still stayed near their ship. They're confused, too, Gary told himself. They don't understand it any more than we do. They're nervous, trying to figure out just what to do.

But they wouldn't stay that way long, he knew.

Shadows flitted in the mushroom forest. Some of the natives, perhaps, sneaking around, keeping under cover, waiting to see what happened.

Caroline spoke from the lock. "The guns aren't any good. They won't work. Just like the voice said."

He nodded, still watching the Hellhounds. She came down the steps and stood beside him.

"We haven't got a chance against them," she said. "They are brutes, strong. They are trained for war. Killing is their business."

The Hellhounds were walking out from their ship, heading cautiously and slowly toward the Earth ship.

"Not too sure of themselves yet," said Gary. "Probably we don't look too formidable to them, but they aren't taking any chances . . . not yet. In a little while they'll figure that we're comparatively harmless and they'll make their play."

The Hellhounds were dog-trotting now, their scaly bodies glistening redly in the sun, their blunt feet lifting little puffs of dust as they ran along.

"What are we going to do, Gary?" Caroline asked.

"Fort up," said Gary. "Fort up and do some thinking. We can't lick these things, hand to hand and rough and tumble. It would be like trying to wrestle a combined alligator and grizzly bear."

"Fort up? You mean the ship."

Gary nodded. "We got to buy us some time. We have to get a thing or two figured out. As it is, we're caught flat-footed."

"What if they find a way of getting at us, even in the ship."

Gary shrugged. "That's a chance we take."

The Hellhounds separated, spreading out to left and right, angling out to come at the ship from two directions.

"You better get into the lock," said Gary. "Grab hold of the closing lever and be ready. When I come, I may have to move fast. There's no telling what these gents are fixing to uncork."

But even as he spoke, the two reptiles charged, angling in at a burst of speed that almost made them blur, a whirlwind of dust spiraling up behind them.

"In we go!" yelled Gary.

He heard Caroline's feet beating a tattoo on the steps. For a split second he stood there, still facing the charging Hellhounds, then whirled and leaped up the steps, catapulting himself into the lock. He saw Caroline swinging the lever down. The ladder ran up into its seat and the lock slammed home. Through its closing edge he caught sight of the beasts as they swung about in a skidding turn, cheated of their kill.

Gary wiped his forehead. "Close thing," he said. "We almost waited too long. I had no idea they could move that fast."

Caroline nodded. "They figured that we wouldn't. They saw a chance to catch us at the very start. Remember how they waddled. That was to make us think that they couldn't move too fast."

The voice said to them: "This is no way to fight."

"It's common sense," said Gary. "Common sense and good strategy."

"What is strategy?"

"Fooling the enemy," said Gary. "Working things so that you get an advantage over him."

"He'll be waiting for you when you come out. And you'll have to come out after a while."

"We rest and take it easy," said Gary, "while he tears up the ground outside and wears himself to a frazzle. And we do some thinking."

"It's a lousy way to fight," the voice insisted.

"Look," said Gary. "Who's doing the fighting here? You or us."

"You, of course," the voice agreed, "but it's still no way to fight."

They sensed the mind withdraw, grumbling to itself.

Gary grinned at Caroline. "Not gory enough to suit him," he said.

Caroline had sat down in a chair and was staring at him, elbow on her knee, chin cupped in her hands.

"We haven't much to work with," she declared. "No electricity. No power. No nothing. This ship is deader than a doornail. It's lucky the lock worked manually or we'd been goners before we even started."

Gary nodded in agreement. "That voice bothers me the most," he said. "It has power, a strange sort of power. It can stop a spaceship dead in its tracks. It can fix guns so that they won't work. It can blanket out electricity; Lord knows what else it can do."

"It can reach into the unknown of space and time," said Caroline. "Into a place no one else could even find and it did that to bring us here."

"It's irresponsible," said Gary. "Back on Earth we'd call it insanity but what you and I would term insanity may be normal here."

"There's no yardstick," said Caroline. "No yardstick to measure sanity. No way in which one can establish a norm for correct behavior or a correct mentality. Maybe the voice is sane. Maybe he has a purpose and a method of arriving at that purpose we do not understand and for that we call him crazy. Every race must be different, must think differently . . . arrive at the same conclusion and the same result, perhaps, but arrive at them differently. You remember all those beings that came to confer with the

Engineers. All of them were capable, perhaps more capable than we. Independently they might have been able to arrive at the same solution as we and perhaps much more easily and more effectively . . . and yet the Engineers sent them home again, because the Engineers could not work with them. Not because they were not capable, but because they thought so differently, because their mental processes ran at such divergent tangents that there was no basis for co-operation."

"And yet we thought like the Engineers," said Gary. "Enough like them, at any rate, that we could work together. I wonder why that is."

Caroline wrinkled her forehead. "Gary, you are certain these goblin things out there are the same race that came to the city of the Engineers?"

"I would swear it," Gary told her. "I got a good look at the one that was there. It sort of . . . well, burned itself into my mind. I'll never quite forget it."

"And the voice," said Caroline. "I wonder if the voice has anything to do with the goblins."

"The goblins," said the voice, "are my pets. Like the dogs and cats you keep. A living thing to keep me from loneliness."

It did not surprise them to hear the voice again and each of them knew then that they had been waiting for it to speak up again.

"But," protested Caroline, "one of the goblins came to the city of the Engineers."

The voice chuckled at them. "Of course, human thing, of course. As my representative, of course. For I must have representatives, don't you see. In a material world, I must be fronted for by something that can be seen . . . that can be perceived. I could not very well go to a meeting of that great importance as a disembodied voice, as a thought stalking the corridors of that empty city. So I sent a goblin and I went along with him."

"What are you, voice?" Caroline asked. "Tell us what you are."

"I still don't think," said the voice, "that what you are doing is a good way to fight a duel. I think you're making a great mistake."

"What makes you think so, Butch?" asked Gary.

"Because," the voice said, "the Hellhounds are building a fire under your ship. It will be just a matter of time until they smoke you out."

Gary and Caroline glanced swiftly at one another, the same thought in their mind.

"No power," said Caroline, weakly.

"The heat absorption units," Gary cried.

"No power," said Caroline. "The absorption cells won't work."

Gary glanced toward the forward vision ports. Thin streamers of smoke were curling up outside the glass.

"The mushrooms burn well," the voice told them, "when they get old and dry. There are lots of old and dry mushrooms around. They'll have no trouble in keeping up the fire."

"Like smoking out a rabbit," said Gary, bitterly.

"You asked for it," the voice declared.

"Get out of here!" yelled Gary. "Get out of here and leave us alone, can't you."

They sensed it leave, mumbling to itself.

Like a bad dream, Gary thought. Like a Wonderland adventure, with he and Caroline the poor bewildered Alice stumbling through a world of vast incredibility.

Listening, they could hear the crackling of the fire. Now the smoke was a dense cloud through the forward ports.

How do you fight when you have no weapon? How do you get out of a spaceship-turned-into-an-oven? How do you think up a smart dodge when your time is numbered in hours, if not, indeed, in minutes?

What are weapons?

How did they start?

What is the basic of a weapon?

"Caroline," Gary asked, "what would you say a weapon was?"

"Why," she told him, "that seems simple to me. An extension of your fist. An extension of your power to hurt, of your ability to kill. Men fought first with tooth and nail and fist and then with stones and clubs. The stones and clubs were extensions of man's fist, an extension of his muscles and his hate or need."

Stones and clubs, he thought. And then a spear. And, after that, a bow. . . .

A bow!

He swung on his heel, walked rapidly back along the ship, jerked open the door to the supply cabinet. Rummaging inside it, he found the things he wanted.

He brought them out, a fistful of wooden flagpoles, each with small flags fastened to one end, the other end steel-tipped for easy sticking in the ground.

"Explorer flags," he explained to Caroline. "You go out on an alien planet and you want to be sure that you can find your way back to the ship. You plant these things at intervals and then follow them back to the ship, picking them up as you go along. No chance of getting lost."

"But . . ." said Caroline.

"Evans figured he was going to use this ship to go to Alpha Centauri. He took some of these things along, just in case."

He placed the steel-shod tip of one of the poles on the floor, threw his weight against the top end. It flexed. Gary grunted in satisfaction.

"A bow?" asked Caroline.

He nodded. "Not too good a one. Not too accurate. Maybe not too strong. When I was a kid I used to go out into the woods and whack me off a sapling. No curve, no nothing. Bigger at one end than the other. But it worked as a bow, after a fashion. Used reeds for arrows. Killed one of my mother's chickens with one once. She whaled me good and proper."

"It's getting warm in here," Caroline told him. "We can't waste any time."

He grinned at her, exuberant now that there was something to do.

"Hunt up some cord," he told her. "Any kind of cord. If it's not strong enough, we'll twist several strands together."

Whistling under his breath, he got to work, tearing the flag off the end of one of the more supple poles, notching either end to hold the cord.

From another stick he split long wands off the straight-grained wood, fashioning them into arrows. There'd be no time for feathering . . . in fact, there were no feathers in the ship, but that was a refinement that would not be needed. He would be using the bow at close range.

But he did have arrowheads. With snippers, he clipped off the sharp tips with which the poles had been shod, drove them into the head of each arrow. Testing them with a finger, he was satisfied. They were sharp enough . . . if he could get some power behind them.

"Gary," said Caroline, and her voice was almost a whimper.

He swung around.

"There's no cord, Gary. I've looked everywhere."

No cord!

"Everywhere?" he asked.

She nodded. "There isn't any. I looked everywhere."

Clothing, he thought, desperately. Strips torn from their clothing. But that would be worse than useless. It would unravel, come apart between his fingers when he needed it the most. Leather? Leather was too stiff to start with, and it would stretch. Wire? Too stiff and no zip to it.

He let the bow-stick fall from his hands, reached up to wipe his face.

"It's getting hot in here," he said.

He twisted around and stared at the forward visors. The smoke was a cloud and there was a ruddy reflection in it, the reflection of the fire that blazed around the ship.

How much longer, he wondered. How much longer before they'd have to open the port and make a dash for it, knowing even as they did that it was a hopeless thing to do, for the Hellhounds would be waiting just outside the port.

The shell of the spaceship crawled with a dull, dead heat, the kind of heat that comes up off a dusty road on a still, hot day in August.

And soon, he knew, it would be a live heat, not a dead heat any longer, but a blasting furnace heat that would pour from every angle of the steel around them, that would shrivel the leather of their shoes and scorch the clothing that they wore. But long before the leather of their shoes shriveled and curled, they would have to make their break, a hopeless dash for freedom that could end in nothing but death at the hands of the things that waited by the port.

Like an oven, like two rabbits roasting in an oven.

We must turn, thought Gary. We must keep turning about so that we will roast evenly on all sides.

"Gary!" cried Caroline.

He swung around.

"Hair?" she asked. "I just thought of it. Would hair make you a bowstring?"

He gasped at the thought. "Hair," he shouted. "Human hair! Why, of course . . . it's the best material there is."

Caroline's hands were busy with her braids. "It's long," she said. "I was proud of it and I let it grow."

"It'll have to be braided," said Gary. "Twisted into a cord."

"Your knife," she said, and he handed it over.

The knife flashed close to her head and one of the braided strands dangled in her hand.

"We'll have to work fast," said Gary. "We haven't got much time."

The air was dry and hard to breath. It burned one's lungs and dried out the tissues of the mouth. When he bent over and placed a hand against the steel plates of the ship's deck, the steel was warm, like the pavement on a summer's day.

"You'll have to help," said Gary. "We have to be fast and sure. We can't afford to bungle. We won't have a second chance."

"Tell me what to do," she said.

Fifteen minutes later, he nodded at her.

"Open the port," he said, "and when you do stand back against the wall. I'll need all the arm room I can get."

He waited, bow in hand, arrow nocked against the cord.

Not much of a bow, he thought. Nothing you would want to try against a willow at three hundred paces. But these things outside aren't willow wands. It will last for a shot or two . . . I hope it lasts for a shot or two.

The port clanged open as Caroline shoved the lever over. Smoke billowed in the opening and in the smoke he saw the bulk of the ones who waited.

He brought the bow up and the wood bent with the sudden surge of hate and triumph that coursed in his being . . . the hate and fear of fire, the hate of things that wait to do a man to death, the fury of a human being backed into a corner by a thing that is not human.

The arrow made a whispering sound and was a silver streak that spurted through the smoke. The bow bent again and there was another whisper, the whisper of cord and wood and the creak of human muscles.

On the ground outside, two dark shapes were threshing in the smoke.

It was just like shooting rabbits.

Chapter Fifteen

"VERY ingenious," said the voice. "You won fair and square. You did much better than I thought you would."

"And now," said Caroline, "you will send us back again. Back to the city of the Engineers."

"Why, certainly," said the voice. "Why, of course, I will. But first, I have to clean up the place. The bodies, first of all. Cadavers are such unsightly things."

Fire puffed briefly and the bodies of the two Hellhounds were gone. A tiny puff of yellow smoke hung over where they had been and a tiny flurry of ashes eddied in the air.

"I asked you once before," said Caroline, "and you didn't tell me. What are you? We looked for signs of culture and . . ."

"You are befuddled, young human," the voice told her. "You seek for childish things. You looked for cities and there are no cities. You looked for roads and ships and farms and there are none of these. You expected to find a civilization and there is no civilization such as you would recognize."

"You are right," said Gary. "There are none of those."

"I have no city," said the voice, "because I need no city. Although I could build a city at a second's notice. The mushroom forests are the only farms I need to feed my little pets. I need no roads and ships because I can go anywhere I wish without the aid of them."

"You mean you can go in your mind," said Caroline.

"In my mind," the voice said. "I go wherever I may wish, in either time or space, and I am there. I do not merely imagine that I am there; I am really there. Long ago my race forsook machines, knowing that in its mental ability, within the depth of its collective mind it had more potentiality than it could ever get from a clattering piece of mechanism. So the race built minds instead of machines. Minds, I say. But mind, one mind, a single mind, is the better explanation. I am that mind today. A single racial mind.

"I used that mind to pluck you from the space-time tunnel at the very moment you were about to emerge above the city of the Engineers. I used that mind to bring the Hellhounds here. That mind grounded your ship and blanketed your guns and that mind could kill you in a moment if I thought the thought."

"But you," said Caroline. "The personal pronoun that you use. The 'I' you speak of. What is that?"

"I am the mind," the voice told them, "and the mind is me. I am the race. I have been the race for many million years."

"And you play God," said Caroline. "You bring lesser things together, into the arena of this world, and you make them fight while you sit and chuckle. . . ."

"Why, of course," the voice said. "Because, you see, I'm crazy. I'm really, at times, quite violently insane."

"Insane!"

"Why, certainly," the voice told them. "It's what would be bound to happen. You can't perfect a mind, a vast communal mind, a mighty racial mind to the point that my mind is perfected and expect it to keep a perfect balance as a good watch would keep perfect time. But the mind's behavior varies. Sometimes," the voice said, quite confidentially, "I'm battier than a bedbug."

"And how are you now?" asked Gary.

"Why, now," the voice said, "as funny as it seems, I'm quite rational. I'm very much myself."

"Then how about fixing it up so that we can get back?"

"Right away," said the voice, very businesslike. "I'll just clean up a thing or two. Don't like the residue of my irrationality cluttering up the planet. That Hellhound ship over there. . . ."

But instead of the Hellhound ship, it was the Earth ship that went skyward in a terrific gout of flame that sent a wash of heat across the barren land.

"Hey, there. . . ." yelled Gary and then stood stock still as the enormity of what had happened crackled in his mind.

"Tsk, tsk," said the voice. "How very stupid of me. How could I have done a thing like that! Now I'll never be able to send you home again."

His cackling laughter filled the sky and beat like a mighty drum.

"The Hellhound ship!" yelled Gary. "Run . . . run . . ."

But even as they whirled to race toward it, it was gone in a blaze of fire, followed by a trail of smoke that hung briefly above the scorched piece of the ground where the ship had lain.

"You couldn't have operated it, anyhow," said the voice. "It wouldn't have done you a single bit of good."

He laughed again and the laughter trailed off into distance, like a retreating thunderstorm.

Gary and Caroline stood side by side and looked at the emptiness of the bog and mushroom forest. A goblin ducked out of a clump of mushrooms and hooted at them, then dashed back in again.

"What do we do?" asked Caroline and it was a question that went echoing down the long corridor of improbability, a question for which there was, at the moment, no satisfactory answer.

Swiftly, Gary made an inventory:

The clothes they stood in.

A few matches in his pocket.

A bow and some arrows, but the bow didn't count for much.

And that was all. There was nothing else.

"More pets," said Caroline, bitterly.

"What's that?" asked Gary, not sure he heard her right.

"Let it go," she said. "Forget I ever said it."

"There's nothing to get hold of," Gary said. "Nothing you can touch. The voice . . . the voice is nothing."

"It's a horrible thing," said Caroline. "Don't you see, Gary, what a horrible thing it is. The tag end of some great race. Think of it. Millions of years, millions of years to build up a mighty mental civilization. Not a mechanical civilization, not a materialistic culture, but a mental civilization. A striving toward understanding rather than toward doing.

"And now it's a senile thing, an insane thing that has gone back to its second childhood, but its power is too great for a child to wield and it is dangerous . . . dangerous."

Gary nodded. "It could masquerade as anything it pleased. It sent one of the goblins to the city of the Engineers and the Engineers thought the goblin was the mentality that they had contacted. But it wasn't. It was a simple, foolish puppet, but the voice moved it as it wished, talked through its flimsy mind."

"The Engineers must have sensed the inherent insanity of that mind," said Caroline. "They may not have been sure, but they must, at least, have sensed it, for they sent it away with all the rest of them. The voice could have worked with us. You notice how it talks the way a human talks . . . that's because it picked our minds, because it found the thoughts and words we used, because it was able to know everything we know."

"It could see everything in the universe," said Gary. "It could know everything that there was to know."

"Perhaps it did," Caroline told him. "Perhaps the weight of the knowledge was too great. When you overload an engine, the engine will burn out. What would happen if you should overload a mind, even a great communal mind such as we have here?"

"Insanity, maybe," said Gary. "Lord, I don't know. It's like nothing I ever ran across before."

Caroline moved close to Gary.

"We're alone, Gary," she said. "The human race stands all alone. No other race has the balance that we have. Other races may be as great, but they do not have the balance. Look at the Engineers. Materialistic, mechanical to a point where they cannot think except along mechanistic lines. And the voice. It goes on the opposite tangent.

No mechanics at all, just mentality. An overwhelming and an awful mentality. And the Hellhounds. Savage killers. Bending every knowledge to the business of killing. Egomaniacs who would destroy the universe to achieve their own supremacy."

They stood silent, side by side. The great red sun was nearing the western horizon. The goblins scuttered through the mushrooms, chirping and hooting. A disgusting thing, a couple of feet long, crawled out of the slimy waters of the bog, reared itself and stared at them, then lumbered around and slid into the water once again.

"I'll start a fire," said Gary. "Night will be coming soon. We'll have to keep the fire going once we get it started. I only have a few matches."

"Maybe we can eat the mushrooms," said Caroline.

"Some of them may be poisonous," Gary told her. "We'll have to watch the goblins. Eat what they eat. No absolute guarantee, of course, that what they eat wouldn't poison us, but it's the only way we have of knowing. We'll eat just a little at a time, only one of us eating . . ."

"The goblins! Do you think they will bother us?"

"Not likely," Gary told her, but he wasn't as confident as he made it sound.

They gathered a stack of the dried stems of the mushrooms and corded them against the night. Gary, carefully shielding the flame with a protecting hand, struck a match and started a small fire.

The sun had set and the stars were coming out in the hazy darkness of the sky . . . but stars they did not know.

They crouched by the fire, more for the companionship of its flames than for the heat it gave, and watched the stars grow brighter, listening to the chattering of the busy goblins in the mushrooms behind them.

"We'll need water," said Caroline.

Gary nodded. "We'll try filtering it. Lots of sand. Sand is a good filter."

"You know," said Caroline, "I can't feel that this has happened to us. I keep thinking, pretty soon we'll wake up and it will be all right. It hasn't really happened. It . . ."

"Gary . . ." she gasped.

He jerked upright at the alarm in her tone.

Her hands were at her head, feeling of the braids of hair.

"It's there again!" she whispered. "The braid I cut off to make a bowstring. I cut it off and it was gone and it is there again!"

"Well, I'll be . . ." But he did not finish the sentence.

For there, not more than a hundred feet away, was the ship . . . Tommy Evans' ship, the ship that the voice had destroyed in a single flash of fire. It sat on the sand sedately, with light pouring from its ports, with the shine of starlight on its plates.

"Caroline!" he shouted. "The ship! The ship!"

"Hurry," said the voice to them. "Hurry, before I change my mind. Hurry, before I go insane again."

Gary reached down a hand and pulled Caroline to her feet.

"Come on," he shouted.

"Think of me as kindly as you can," said the voice. "Think of me as an old man, an old, old man, who is not quite the man he was . . . not quite the man he was."

They ran, stumbling in the darkness, toward the ship.

"Hurry, hurry," the voice shouted at them. "I cannot trust myself."

"Look!" cried Caroline. "Look, in the sky!"

The wheel of light was there, the slow, lazy wheel of light they first had seen on Pluto . . . the entrance to the space-time tunnel.

"I gave you back the ship," said the voice. "I gave you back the strand of hair. Think kindly of me please . . . think kindly . . ."

They clambered up the ladder to the open port and slammed the lock behind them.

At the controls, Gary reached out for the warming knob, found that it was already turned on. The tubes, the indicator said, were warm.

He gunned the ship into the sky, centering the cross hairs on the wheel that shimmered above them.

They hit it head-on and the black closed in around them and then there was light again and the city of the Engineers was below them . . . a blasted city, its proud towers gone, great heaps of rubble in its streets, a cloud of stone-dust, ground in the mills of atomic bombing, hanging over it.

Gary glanced over his shoulder, triumphant at their return, and saw the tears that welled in Caroline's eyes and trickled down her cheeks.

"The poor thing," she said. "That poor old man back there."

Chapter Sixteen

THE city of the Engineers lay in ruins, but above it, fighting desperately, battling valiantly to hold off the hordes of Hellhounds, the tiny remnant of the Engineer battle fleet still stood between it and complete destruction.

The proud towers were blasted into dust and the roadways and parks were sifted with the white cloud of destruction, the powdered masonry smashed and pulverized to drifting fragments by the disintegrator rays and the atomic bombs. Twisted bits of wreckage littered the chaotic wastes of shattered stone—wreckage of Engineer and Hellhound ships that had met in the shock of battle and plunged in flaming ruin.

Gary glanced skyward anxiously. "I hope they can hold them off," he said, "long enough for the energy to build up."

Caroline straightened from the bank of instruments mounted upon the roof outside the laboratory.

"It's building up fast," she said. "I'm almost afraid. It might get out of control, you know. But we have to have enough energy to start with. If the first stroke doesn't utterly destroy the Hellhounds, we won't have a second chance."

Gary's mind ran over the hectic days of work, the mad scramble against time. He remembered once again how Kingsley and Tommy had gone out to the edge of the universe to create a huge bubble of space-time, warping the rim of space into a hump, curving the time-space continuum into a hypersphere that finally closed and divorced itself from the parent body, pinching off like a yeast bud to become an independent universe in the inter-space.

It had taken power to do that, a surging channel of energy that poured out of the magnetic power transmitter, crossing space in a tight beam to be at hand for the making of a new universe. But it had taken even more power to "skin" a hypersphere, to turn it through a theoretical fifth dimension until it was of the stuff that the inter-space was made of—a place where time did not exist, a place whose laws were not the laws of the universe, a mystery region that was astonishingly easy to maneuver through space once it was created. It wasn't a sphere or a hypersphere— it was a strange dimension that apparently did not lend itself to measurement, or to definition, or to identification by any of the normal senses of perception.

But whatever it was, it hung there above the city, although there was no clue to its existence. It couldn't be seen or sensed—just something that had been created from equations supplied by the last man living out his final days on a dying planet, equations that Caroline had scribbled on the back of a crumpled envelope. An envelope, Gary remembered, that had carried an irate letter from a creditor back on Earth who felt that he should have long since been paid. "Too long overdue," the letter had said. Gary grinned. Back on Earth the creditor undoubtedly still was sending him letters pointing out that the account was becoming longer overdue with the passing of each month.

Outside the universe that tiny, created hypersphere was bumping along, creating frictional stress, creating a condition for the creation of the mysterious energy of eternity —an energy that even now was pouring into the universe and being absorbed by the fifth-dimensional frame that poised above the city.

A new, raw energy from a region that had no time, an energy that was at once timeless and formless, but an energy that was capable of being crystallized into any form.

Kingsley was standing beside Gary, his great head bent, staring upward. "An energy field," he said, "and what energy! Like a battery, storing up that energy from inter-space. I hope it does what Caroline thinks it will."

"Don't worry," said Gary. "You saw the mathematics that she brought back."

"Sure, I saw the mathematics," Kingsley said, "but I couldn't understand them."

He shook his head inside the helmet.

"What's the universe coming to?" he asked.

Caroline spoke quietly to the Engineer.

"There's plenty of energy now," she said. "You may call them down."

The Engineer, headphones clamped upon his skull, apparently was giving orders to the Engineer fleet, but the Earthlings couldn't catch his thoughts.

"Watch now," chirped Herb. "This is going to be a sight worth seeing."

High above the city a ship dropped, flashing downward, like a silver bullet. Another dropped and still another, until the entire Engineer fleet, blackened and ripped and decimated, was in full retreat, flashing back toward the ruined city. And in their wake came the triumphant Hellhounds, a victorious pack in full cry, determined to wipe out the last trace of a hated civilization.

The Engineer had snatched the headphones off, was racing to the set of controls. Gary, glancing from the battle scene above, saw his metal fingers reach out and manipulate controls, saw Caroline pick up an ordinary flashlight.

He knew that the Engineer was shifting the fifth-dimensional mass into a position between them and the screaming fleet of death above them, shifting that field of terrible energy into the Hellhounds' path.

The last of the Engineer fleet had reached the city, was shrieking down between the shattered towers, as if fleeing for its very life.

And only a few miles above them, in what amounted to a mass formation, the Hellhound fleet was plunging down, guns silent now, protective screens still up, grim and ghastly ships running their quarry to the ground.

Gary's body tensed as he saw Caroline's arm swing up, clutching the tiny flashlight, pointing it at the on-driving fleet.

He saw the flash of light burn upward, pale in the light

of the sinking suns—a tiny, feeble, ineffective beam of light stabbing at the oncoming ships. Like taking a swipe at a grizzly bear with a pancake turner.

And then the heavens seemed to blaze with light and a streamer of blue-white intensity whipped out toward the ships. Protective screens flared briefly and then exploded into a million flashing sparks. For the space of one split second, before he could get his hand up to shield his eyes against the inferno in the sky, Gary saw the gaunt black skeletons of the Hellhound ships, writhing and disappearing in the surging blast of energy that tore at them and twisted them and finally, in the snapping of one's finger, utterly destroyed them.

The sky was empty, as empty as if there had never been a Hellhound ship. There was no sign of the fifth-dimensional mass, no hint of ship or gun—just the blue of the sky, ashing into violet as the three suns swung below the far-off horizon.

"Well," said Herb, and Gary could hear his voice sobbing with excitement, "that's the end of the Hellhounds."

Yes, that was the end of the Hellhounds, thought Gary. There was nothing in the universe that could stand before such a blast of energy. When the light, the tiny, feeble beam from the ridiculous little flash had struck the energy field, the energy, that timeless, formless stuff, had suddenly crystallized, had taken on the form of the energy that it had encountered. And in a burst of light it had struck at the Hellhounds, struck with terrible effectiveness —with entire lack of mercy, had wiped them out in the winking of one's eye.

He tried to imagine that blast of light moving out into the universe. It would travel for years, would flash its merciless way for many thousands of light-years. In time its energy would wane, would slowly dissipate, would lose some of its power in the vast spaces of intergalactic space. And perhaps the day would come when all its energy would be gone. But meanwhile nothing could stand in its way, nothing could resist it. In years to come great suns might explode into invisible gas as the frightful beam of power reached them and annihilated them and then passed on. And some astronomer, catching the phenomena in his lens, would speculate upon just what had happened.

He turned slowly around and faced Caroline. "How does it feel," he asked, "to win a war?"

The face she turned to him was strained and worn. "Don't say that to me," she said. "I had to do it. They were a terrible race, but they were alive—and there is so little life in this universe."

"You need some sleep," he said.

He saw the tragic lines of her mouth.

"There is no sleep," she said. "No rest at all. We have just started. We have to save the universe. We have to create more and more of the fifth-dimensional frameworks, many of them and larger. To absorb the energy when the universes meet."

Gary started. He had forgotten the approaching universe. So absorbed had they become in ending the Hellhound attack that the edge of the real and greater danger had been dulled.

But now, brought back to it, he realized the job they faced.

He spun on the Engineer. "How much longer?" he asked. "How much longer have we?"

"Very little time," said the Engineer. "Very little. I fear that energy may flood in upon us at any time."

"That energy," said Kingsley, a fanatical flame in his eyes. "Think of what could be done with it. We could set up a huge framework of fifth-dimensional space, use it as an absorber, a battery. We could send energy almost anywhere throughout the universe. A central universal power plant."

"First," declared Tommy, "you'd have to control it, be able to direct it in a tight beam."

"First," insisted Caroline, "we have to do something about this other universe."

"Wait a second," said Gary. "We've forgotten something. We asked those people in the other universe to come over and help us, but we don't need them now."

He looked at the Engineer. "Have you heard from them?" he asked.

"Yes," said the Engineer. "I have heard from them. They still want to come."

"They still want to come?" Astonishment rang in Gary's voice. "Why should they want to come?"

"They want to emigrate to our universe," said the Engineer. "And I have agreed to allow them to do so."

"You have agreed?" rumbled Kingsley. "And since when has this universe been in the market for immigrants? We don't know what kind of people they are. They might be dangerous. They may want to destroy the present life within the universe."

"There is plenty of room for them," said the Engineer, and if possible, his voice seemed colder and more impersonal than ever. "There is room to spare. We have over fifty billion galaxies and more than fifty billion stars in each galaxy. Only one out of every ten thousand of the stars has a solar system, that is true, of course . . . but only one out of every hundred solar systems has life. And if we need more solar systems we can manufacture them. With the power of the dimension of eternity at our command, we can move stars, we can hurl them together to make solar systems. With this power we can reshape the universe, mold it to our needs."

The idea impacted with stunning force on Gary's brain. They could reshape the universe! Working with the raw materials at hand, with the almost infinite power at their command, they could alter the course of stars, could realign the galaxies, could manufacture planets, set up a well coordinated plan to offset entropy, the tendency to run down, the tendency to go amuck. His mind groped futilely at the ideas, pawing them over and over, but back of it all was a curtain of wonderment and awe. And through his brain sang a subtle warning . . . a persistent little warning that hammered at his thoughts. Mankind itself wasn't ready for such power, couldn't use it intelligently, perhaps would destroy the universe with it. Was there any other entity in the universe qualified to use it? Would it be wise to place such power in the hands of any entity?

"But why," Caroline was asking, "do they want to come?"

"Because," said the Engineer, "we are going to destroy their universe to save ours."

It was as if a bombshell had been dropped among them. Silence clapped down. Gary felt Caroline's hand creep into his. He held it tight.

"But why destroy their universe?" shouted Tommy. "We have the means at hand to save them both. All we have to do is create more of those five-dimensional screens to absorb the energy."

"No," said the Engineer, "we cannot do it. Given time, we could. But there is so little time, not nearly enough. The energy would overwhelm us once it came. It would take so many screens and we have so little time."

His thoughts cut off and Gary heard the shuffle of Kingsley's feet.

"These other beings," the Engineer went on, "know that their universe has very little longer to exist in any event. It has almost reached the end of its time. It soon will die the heat death. Throughout its space, matter and energy are being swiftly distributed. Soon the day will arrive when it will be equally distributed, when the heat, the energy, the mass throughout the universe will be spread so thin that it scarcely exists."

Gary sucked in his breath. "Like a watch running down," he said.

"You're right," said Kingsley. "Like a watch that has run down. That is what will happen to our universe in time."

"Not," said Gary, "if we have the energy from interspace at our command."

"Already," said the Engineer, "only one corner of this other universe is still suitable for life . . . the area that is facing us. Into that corner all life has been driven and now it has been, or is being, assembled to transfer itself to our universe."

"But," asked Herb, "just how are they going to get here?"

"They will use a time warp," said the Engineer. "They will bud out from their universe, but in doing so they will distort the time factor in the walls of their hypersphere . . . a distortion that will send them ahead in time, will push their little universe closer to us than to their universe. Our gravity will grasp their hypersphere and draw it in."

"But that," protested Gary, "will produce more energy. Their little universe will be destroyed."

"No," declared the Engineer, "because they will merge their space-time continuum with the continuum of our universe as soon as the two come together. They will immediately become a part of our universe."

"You told them how to create a hypersphere?" asked Herb.

"I did," said the Engineer. "And it will save the people of that other universe. They had tried many things, had worked out theories and new branches of mathematics in their efforts to escape. They discovered many things that we do not know, but they never thought of budding out from their universe. They apparently are a mechanistic people, a people very much like we Engineers. They seem to have lost that vital spark of imagination with which your people are so well supplied."

"My Lord," said Gary, "think of it! Imagination saving the people of another universe. The imagination of a little third-rate race that hasn't even started really using its imagination yet."

"You are right," declared the Engineer, "and in the aeons to come that imagination will make your race the masters of the entire universe."

"Prophesy," said Gary.

"I know," said the Engineer.

"There's just one thing," said Herb. "How is that other universe going to be destroyed?"

"We are going to destroy it," said the Engineer, "in exactly the same way we destroyed the Hellhounds."

Chapter Seventeen

TOMMY sat in the pilot's seat and urged the ship slowly forward, using rocket blast after rocket blast to keep it on its course.

vicious bombs, impregnable to anything . . . to anything except the flashlight in the hands of a wisp of a girl.

Remembering that, it was easier to believe that the disintegrators, crystalizing a much vaster field of energy, might accomplish the destruction of a universe. For it wasn't the guns themselves that would do the job, but the direction of all the energy into the other universe, energy rising on the million-mile front set up by the fanning guns.

"The field is building up," said Caroline. "Be ready."

Gary grinned at her. "We'll fire when we see the whites of their eyes," he said.

He racked his brain for the origin of that sentence. Something out of history. Something out of the dim old legends of the past. A folk tale of some mighty battle of the ancient days.

He shrugged his shoulders. The story, whatever it might be, probably wasn't true, anyhow. So few of the ancient legends were. Just another story to be told of a black night in the chimney corner when the wind howled around the eaves and the rain dripped on the roof.

His eyes went to the port again, stared out into the misty blue, the blue that seemed to throb with vibrant life.

They had to wait. Wait until the energy had built up to a point where it would be effective. But not too long. For if they waited too long, it might pour into their own universe and wipe them out.

"Get ready," thundered Kingsley, and Gary's hand went out to the switch that would loosen the blast of the disintegrator. His fingers gripped the switch tightly, tensed, ready for action.

"Give it to 'em," Kingsley roared, and Gary snapped the switch.

With both hands he swung the swivel back and forth, back and forth. Beside him, he knew, Herb was doing the same.

Outside the port blossomed a maelstrom of fiery light, a blinding, vicious flare of light that seemed to leap and writhe and then become a solid sheet of flame. A solid sheet of flame that drove on and on, leaping outward, bringing doom to a worn-out universe.

It was over in just a few seconds . . . a few seconds during which an inferno of energy was turned loose to rage between two universes.

Then the misty blue filled the port again and the ship was bucking, tossed about like a chip in heavy seas, twisted and dashed about by the broken lines of force that still heaved and quivered under the backlash of the titanic forces which a moment before had filled the inter-space.

Gary turned in his seat, saw that Caroline and the Engineer were bent over the detector dial, watching it intently.

Kingsley, looking over the Engineer's shoulder, was muttering: "No sign. No sign of energy."

That meant, then, that the other universe was already contracting, was rushing backward to a new beginning . . . no longer a menace.

Gary patted the gun. It and Man's ingenuity had turned the trick. Mere Man had destroyed one universe, but had saved another. It seemed too utterly fantastic to be true.

He looked around the control room. Tommy at the controls. Herb at the second gun. The other three watching the energy detector. Everything was familiar. Nothing was any different than it was before. All commonplace and ordinary.

And yet, for the first time, tiny beings spawned within the universe, had taken firm hold of the universe's destiny. Henceforward Man and his little compatriots throughout the vast gulfs of space would no longer be mere pawns in the grim tide of cosmic forces. Henceforward life would rule these forces, bend them to its will, put them to work, change them, shift them about.

Life was an accident. There was little doubt of that. Something that wasn't exactly planned. Something that had crept in, like a malignant disease in the ordered mechanism of the universe. The universe was hostile to life. The depths of space were too cold for life, most of the condensed matter too hot for life, space was traversed by radiations inimical to life. But life was triumphant. In the end, the universe would not destroy it . . . it would rule the universe.

His mind went back to the day Herb had sighted that

"You have to fight to stand still here," he gritted between his teeth. "A man can't tell just where he is. There doesn't seem to be any direction, nothing to orient oneself."

"Of course not," rumbled Kingsley. "We're in a sort of place no other man has ever been. We're right out in the area where space and time are breaking down, where lines of force are all distorted, where everything is jumbled and broken up."

"The edge of the universe," said Caroline.

Gary stared out through the vision plate. There was nothing to see, nothing but a deep blue void that queerly seemed alive with a deep intensity of life.

He turned from the panel and asked the Engineer: "Any signs of energy yet?"

"Faint signs," said the Engineer, bending lower to peer at the dial set in a detector instrument. "Very faint signs. The other universe is almost upon us now and the lines of force are just beginning to make themselves felt."

"How much longer will it take?" asked Kingsley.

"I cannot tell," said the Engineer. "We know very little about the laws out here. It may be a very short while or it may be some time as yet."

"Well," said Herb, "the fireworks can start any time now. The folks from the other universe have crossed safely and there's no reason for the other universe to exist. We can blast it any time we want to."

"Gary," said Kingsley, "you and Herb better get over to those guns. We may want action fast."

Gary nodded and walked to the controls of a disintegrator gun. He slid into the seat back of the controls and reached out a hand to grasp the swivel butt. He swung it back and forth, knew that outside the ship the grim muzzle of the weapon was swinging in a wide arc.

Through the tiny port in front of him he could see the blue intensity of the void in which they moved.

Out here time and space were thinning down and breaking up. Like a boat riding on the surface of a heaving sea, they were riding the very rim of the universe, their ship tossed about by the shifting, twisting co-ordinates of force.

Out there somewhere, very close, was the mysterious

inter-space. Close, too, invisible in all its immensity, was another universe. An old and tottering universe from which its inhabitants had fled, a dying universe that had been sentenced to death so that a younger universe might live.

In just a few minutes now the space between the universes would begin to fill with a charge of that terrible timeless, formless energy. Slowly it would begin seeping into the two universes, slowly at first and then faster and faster, increasing their mass, dooming them to almost instant destruction.

But before that could happen, the disintegrator ray, the most terrible form of energy known to the Engineers, would blast out into that field of latent energy, would sweep outward toward that other approaching universe.

Instantly the field of energy would be turned into the terrific power of the disintegrator ray, but millions of times more powerful than the ray itself . . . a blinding sheet of energy that would stop at nothing, that would smash the very mold of time and space, would destroy matter and cancel other energy. And this sheet of energy would smash its way into the other universe.

And when that happened, the energy field, draining all its energy into the disintegrator blast, would be diverted from the younger universe, would turn in full force upon the one to be destroyed.

Staggering under the onrush of such a fierce storm of energy, the old universe would start contracting. Its mass would build up, faster and faster, as the fifth-dimensional energy, riding on the beams of the disintegrator guns, hurled itself into its space-time frame.

Gary wiped his brow with the back of his hand.

That was the way Caroline and the Engineer had figured it out. He hoped that it would work. And yet it seemed impossible that a tiny ship, two tiny guns manned by the puny members of the human race, could utterly annihilate a universe, an unimaginably massive space-time matrix.

Yet he had seen the beam of a tiny flashlight, crystalizing the energy of the eternal dimension, blast out of existence, in the twinkling of an eye, a mighty fleet of warships protected by heavy screens, armored against tiny flash of reflected light in the telescopic screen . . . back to the finding of the girl in the space shell. And before him seemed to unreel the chain of events that had led up to this moment. If Caroline Martin had not been condemned to space, if she had not known the secret of suspended animation, if that suspended animation had not failed to suspend thought, if Herb had not seen the flash that revealed the presence of the shell, if he, himself, had been unable to revive the girl, if Kingsley had not been curious about why cosmic rays should form a definite pattern . . .

And in that chain of happenings he seemed to see the hand of something greater than just happenstance. What was it the old man back on Old Earth had said? Something about a great dreamer creating stages and peopling them with actors.

"No energy indications," said the Engineer. "We have definitely ended the menace. The other universe has contracted beyond the danger point. We are saved. I am so very happy."

He faced them. "And so very grateful, too," he said.

"Forget it," said Herb. "It was our neck as well as yours."

Chapter Eighteen

HERB polished the last chicken bone methodically and sighed. "That's the best meal I ever ate," he said.

They sat at the table in the apartment the Engineers had arranged for them. It had escaped the general destruction of the Hellhound attack, although the tower above it had been obliterated by a hydrogen bomb.

Gary filled his wineglass again and leaned back in his chair.

"I guess our job is done here," he said. "Maybe we'll be going home in just a little while."

"Home?" asked Caroline. "You mean the Earth?"

Gary nodded.

"I have almost forgotten the Earth," she said. "It has been so long since I have seen the Earth. I suppose it has changed a great deal since I saw it last."

"Perhaps it has," Gary told her, "although there are some things that never change. The smell of fresh-plowed fields and the scent of hayfields at harvest time and the beauty of trees against the skyline at evening."

"Just a poet," said Herb. "Just a blasted poet."

"Maybe there will be things I won't recognize," said Caroline. "Things that will be so different."

"I'll show you the Earth," said Gary. "I'll set you straight on everything."

"What bothers me," declared Kingsley, "are those people from the other universe. It's just like letting undesirable elements come in under our immigration schedule on Earth. You can't tell what sort of people they are. They might be life forms that are inimical to us."

"Or," suggested Caroline, "they might be possessors of great scientific accomplishments and a higher culture. They might add much to this universe."

"There isn't much danger from them," said Gary. "The Engineers are taking care of them. They're keeping them cooped up in the hypersphere they used to cross interspace until suitable places for their settlement can be found. The Engineers will keep an eye on them."

Metallic feet grated on the floor and Engineer 1824 came across the room toward the table.

He stopped before the table and folded his arms across his chest.

"Everything is all right?" he asked. "The food is good and you are comfortable."

"I'll say we are," said Herb.

"We are glad," said the Engineer. "We have tried so hard to make it easy for you. We are grateful that you came. Without you we never would have saved the universe. We never would have gone to Old Earth to find the secret of the energy, because we are not driven by restless imagination . . . an imagination that will not let one rest until all has been explained."

"We did what we could," rumbled Kingsley. "But all of the credit goes to Caroline. She was the one who worked out the mathematics for the creation of the hypersphere. She is the only one of us who would have been able to understand the equations relating to the energy and the inter-space."

"You are right," said the Engineer, "and we thank Caroline especially. But the rest of you had your part to do and did it. It has made us very proud."

"Proud," thought Gary. "Why should he be proud of anything we've done?"

The Engineer caught his thought.

"You ask why we should be proud," he said, "and I shall tell you why. We have watched and studied you closely since you came, debating whether you should be told what there is to tell. Under different circumstances we probably would allow you to depart without a word, but we have decided that you should know."

"Know what?" thundered Kingsley.

The rest of them were silent, waiting.

"You are aware of how your solar system came into being?" asked the Engineer.

"Sure," said Kingsley. "There was a dynamic encounter between two stars. Our Sun and an invader. About three billion years ago."

"That invader," said the Engineer, "was the Sun of my people, a sun upon whose planets they had built a great civilization. My people knew well in advance that the collision would take place. Our astronomers discovered it first and after that our physicists and other scientists worked unceasingly in a futile effort either to avert the collision or to save what could be salvaged of our civilization when the encounter came. But century after century passed, with the two stars swinging closer and closer together. There seemed no chance to save anything. We knew that the planets would be destroyed when the first giant tide from your Sun lashed out into space, that the resultant explosion would instantly destroy all life, that more than likely some of the planets would be totally destroyed.

"Our astronomers told us that our Sun would pass within two million miles of your star, that it would grip and drag far out in space some of the molten mass which your Sun would eject. In such a case we could see but little hope for the continuance of our civilization."

His thoughts broke off, but no one said a word. All eyes were staring at the impassive metal face of the Engineer, waiting for him to continue.

"Finally, knowing that all their efforts were hopeless, my people constructed vast spaceships. Spaceships designed for living, for spending many years in space. And long before the collision occurred these ships were launched, carrying select groups of our civilization. Representative groups. Men of different sciences, with many records of our civilization."

"The Ark," said Caroline, breathlessly. "The old story of the Ark."

"I do not understand," said the Engineer.

"It doesn't matter," Caroline said. "Please go on."

"From far out in space my people watched the two stars sweep past each other," said the Engineer. "It was as if the very heavens had exploded. Great tongues of gas and molten matter speared out into space for millions of miles. They saw their own Sun drag a great mass of this stellar material for billions of miles out into space, strewing fragments of it en route. They saw the gradual formation of the matter around your Sun and then, in time, they lost sight of it, for they were moving far out into space and the eruptive masses were settling down into a quieter state.

"For generation after generation, my people hunted for a new home. Men died and were given burial in space. Children were born and grew old in turn and died. For century after century the great ships voyaged from star to star, seeking a planetary system on which they might settle and make their homes. One of the ships ran too close to a giant sun and was drawn to its death. Another was split wide open when it collided with a dark star. But the rest braved the dangers and uncertainties of space, hunting, always hunting for a home."

Another pause and still there were no questions. The Engineer went on:

"But no planetary system could be found. Only one star in every ten thousand has a planetary system, and they might have hunted for thousands of years without finding one.

"Finally, tired out with searching, they decided to return to your Sun. For while there was as yet no planetary system there, they knew that in ages to come there would be."

The cold wind from space was flicking Gary in the face again. Could this tale the Engineer was telling be the truth? Was this why the Engineers had been signaling to Pluto?

The Engineer's thoughts were coming again.

"After many years they reached your Sun, and as they approached it they saw that planets were beginning to form around the centers of relatively dense matter. But there was something else. Swinging in a great, erratic orbit on the very edge of this nebula-like mass of raw planetary matter was a planet which they recognized. It was one of the planets of their old home star, fourth out from their Sun. It had been stolen from their Sun, now was swinging in an orbit of its own around its adopted star.

"My people had found a home at last. They descended to the surface of the planet to find that its atmosphere was gone, that all life had vanished, that all signs of civilization had been utterly wiped out.

"But they settled there and tried to rebuild, in part at least, the civilization that was their heritage. But it was a heart-rending task. For years and centuries they watched the slow formation of your solar system, saw the planets take on shape and slowly cool, waiting against the day when the race might occupy them. But the process was too slow. The work of building their civilization anew, the lack of atmosphere, the utter cold of space, were sapping the strength of my people. They foresaw the day when they would perish, when the last one of the race would die. But they planned for the future. They planned very carefully.

"They created us and gave us great ships and sent us out to try to find them new homes, hoping against hope that we would be able to find them a better home before it was too late. For out in space our ships separated, each traveling its own way, bent on a survey of the entire universe if such were necessary."

"They created you?" asked Gary. "What do you mean?

Aren't you direct descendants of that other race, the race of the invading star?"

"No," said the Engineer. "We are robots. But so carefully made, so well endowed with a semblance of life that we cannot be distinguished from authentic life forms. I sometimes think that in all these years we may have become life in all reality. I have thought about it a great deal, have hoped so much that we might in time become something more than mere machines."

In the silence, Gary wondered why he had not guessed the truth before. It had been there to see. The form, the very actions of the Engineers were mechanistic. Once the Engineer had told them that he was bound by mechanistic precepts, that he and his fellows possessed almost no imagination. And machines, of course, would have no imagination.

But they had seemed so much like people, almost like human beings, that he had thought of them as actual life, but cast in metallic rather than protoplasmic form.

"Well, I'll be damned," said Kingsley.

"Boy," said Herb, "you're topnotch robots, if I do say so."

Gary snarled at him across the table. "Pipe down," he warned.

"Maybe you aren't robots any more," Caroline was saying. "Maybe through all these years you have become real entities. Your creators must have given you electrochemical brains, and that, after all, is what the human brain amounts to. In time those brains would become real, almost as efficient, probably in some instances even more efficient than a protoplasmic brain. And brain power, the ability to think and reason, seems to be all that counts when everything is balanced out."

"Thank you," said the Engineer. "Thank you very much. You are so kind to say so. That is what I have tried to tell myself."

"Look here," said Gary. "It really doesn't matter, does it? I mean, whether you are robots or independent entities. You serve the same purpose, you follow the same dictates of conscience, you create the same destiny as things that move and act through the very gift of life. In many ways, to my mind, a robotic existence might be preferable to a human existence."

"Perhaps it doesn't really matter," agreed the Engineer. "I told you once that we were a proud people, that we had inherited a great trust, that we had carried out that trust. Pride might have kept us from telling you what we were, but now I am glad I have, for the rest will be easier to understand."

"The rest," said Tommy in surprise. "Is there more?"

"Much more," said the Engineer.

"Wait a second," rumbled Kingsley. "Do you mean that all you Engineers were created by a race that flourished three billion years ago, that you have lived through that space of time?"

"Not all of us," said the Engineer. "My people made only a few of us, a few to man each ship. We ourselves have made others, copies of ourselves. But in each new creation we have tried to inculcate some of the factors which we find missing in ourselves. Imagination, for one thing, and greater initiative, and a greater scope of emotional perception."

"You yourself are one of the original robots made back on Pluto?" asked Caroline.

The Engineer nodded.

"You are eternal and immortal," suggested Kingsley.

"Not eternal nor immortal," said the Engineer. "But with proper care, replacement of worn-out parts, and barring accident, I will continue to function for many more billions of years to come."

Billions of years, thought Gary. It was something a man could not imagine. A human mind could not visualize a billion years or a thousand years or even a hundred years. Man, in general, could visualize not much beyond the figure four.

But if the Engineers had lived for three billion years, how come they had been unable to create a hypersphere, why hadn't they probed out beyond the universe to learn the laws of inter-space? Why must this work wait for the arrival of the human mind?

"I have answered that before," said the Engineer, "and I will answer it again. It is because of imagination and vision . . . the ability to see beyond facts, to probe into probabilities, to visualize what might be and then attempt to make it so. That is something that we cannot do. We are chained to mechanistic action and mechanistic thought. We do not advance beyond the proven fact. When two facts create another fact, we accept the third fact, but we do not reach out in speculation, collect half a dozen tentative facts and then try to crystallize them. That is the answer to your question."

Gary looked startled. He hadn't realized that the Engineer could read his undirected thoughts. Caroline was looking at him, a smile twitching the corners of her mouth.

"Did you ask him something?"

"I guess I did," said Gary.

"Did you ever hear from the other Engineers?" asked Kingsley. "The ones who were in the other ships?"

"No," said the Engineer, "we never did. Presumably they have by now found other planets where they are doing the same work as we. We have tried to get in touch with them, but we have never been able to do it."

"What is your work?" asked Gary.

"Why," said Caroline, "you should know that, Gary. It is to prepare a place for the Engineers' people to live. Isn't that right?" she asked the Engineer.

"It is right," said the Engineer.

"But," protested Gary, "those people are dead. There is no sign of them in our solar system and they certainly didn't start out looking for some other planet. They died off on Pluto."

He remembered the chiseled masonry that Ted Smith had found. The hands of the Engineers' creators had cut those stones, billions of years ago . . . and today they still were on Pluto's surface, mute testimony to the greatness of a race that had died while the solar system's planets still were cooling off.

"They are not dead," said the Engineer, and his thoughts seemed to have a particular warmth in them.

"Not dead," said Gary. "Do you know where they are?"

"Yes," said the Engineer. "I do. Some of them are in this very room."

"In this room," began Caroline, and then she stopped

as the significance of what the Engineer had said struck home.

"In this room," said Herb. "Hell, the only people who are in this room are us. And we aren't your people."

"But you are," declared the Engineer. "There are differences, to be sure. But you are much like them, so like them in many ways. You are protoplasmic and they were protoplasmic. Your general form is the same and, I have no doubt, your metabolism. And above all, the way your mind works."

"That," said Caroline, "was why we could understand you and you could understand us. Why you kept us here when you sent the other entities back to their homes."

"Do you mean," asked Kingsley, "that we are the direct descendants of your people . . . that your people finally took over the planets? That seems hardly possible, for we know we started from very humble beginnings. We have no legends, no evidence pointing to such a genesis."

"Not that," said the Engineer. "Not exactly that. But I suppose you have wondered how life got its start on your planet. There are many planetary systems, you know, where life is entirely unknown. Planets that are fully as old as yours that are barren of all life."

"There is the spore theory," said Kingsley, and as he said the words he pounded the table with his massive fist.

"By Lord, that's it," he shouted. "The spore theory. Your people out on Pluto, only a few of them left, with the planets still unfit for habitation, knowing that they faced the end . . . couldn't they have insured life on the young planets by the development and planting of life spores?"

"That," said the Engineer, "is what I thought. That is the theory that I hold."

"But if that were the case," objected Caroline, "why should we have developed as we did? Why should a life form almost duplicating the Engineers' people have developed? Surely they couldn't have planted determinants in the spore . . . they couldn't have seen or planned that far ahead. They couldn't possibly have planned the eventual evolution of a race re-creating their own!"

"They were a very ancient people," said the Engineer,

"and a very clever people. I do not doubt that they could have planned it as you say."

"Interesting," said Herb. "But what does it make us?"

"It makes you the heir of my people," said the Engineer. "It means that what we have done here, all we have, all we know is yours. We will rebuild this city, we will condition it in such a manner that your people can live here. Also that whatever the other Engineers may have found or done is yours. We want nothing for ourselves except the joy and the satisfaction of knowing that we have served, that we have done well with the trust that was handed to us."

They sat stunned, scarcely believing what they heard.

"You mean," asked Kingsley, "that you will rebuild this city and hand it over to the people of our solar system?"

"That is what I mean," said the Engineer. "It is yours. I have no doubt that you descended in some manner from my people. Since you came here I have studied you closely. Time and again I have seen little actions and mannerisms, little mental quirks that mark you as being in some way connected with the people who created us."

Gary tried to reason it out. The Engineers were handing the human race a heritage from an ancient people, handing them a city and a civilization already built, a city and a civilization such as the race itself would not achieve for the next many thousand years.

But there was something wrong, something that didn't click.

He remembered Herb's comment that the city looked like a place that was waiting for someone who had never come. Herb had hit upon the exact situation. This city had been built for a greater race, for a race that probably had died long before the first stone had been laid in place. A race that must have been so far advanced that it would make the human race look savage in comparison.

He tried to imagine what effect such a city and such a civilization would have upon the human race. He tried to picture the greed and hate, the political maneuvering, the fierce trade competition, the social inequality and its resultant class struggle . . . all of it inherent in humanity . . .

in this white city under the three suns. Somehow the two didn't go together.

"We can't do it," he said. "We aren't ready yet. We'd just make a mess of things. We'd have too much power, too much leisure, too many possessions. It would smash our civilization and leave us one in its stead that we could not manage. We haven't put our own civilization upon a basis that could coincide with what is here."

Kingsley stared at him.

"But think of the scientific knowledge! Think of the cultural advantages!" he shouted.

"Gary is right," said Caroline. "We aren't ready yet."

"Sometime," said Gary. "Sometime in the future. When we have wiped out some of the primal passions. When we have solved the great social and economic problems that plague us now. When we have learned to observe the Golden Rule . . . when we have lost some of the lustiness of our youth. Sometime we will be ready for this city."

He remembered the ancient man they had met on Old Earth. He had said something about the rest of the race going away, to a far star, to a place that had been prepared for them.

That place the old man had spoken of, he realized now, was this very city. And that meant that the Old Earth they had visited had been the real Earth . . . no shadow planet, but the actuality existing in the future. And the old man had spoken as if the rest of the race had gone to the city but a short while earlier. He had said that he refused to go, that he couldn't leave the Earth.

The time would be long, then. Longer than he thought. A long and bitter wait for the day when the race might safely enter into a better world, into a heritage left to them by a race that died when the solar system was born.

"You understand?" he asked the Engineer.

"I understand," the Engineer replied. "It means that we must wait for the masters that we worked for . . . that it will be long before they come to us."

"You waited three billion years," Gary reminded him. "Wait a few million more for us. It won't take us long. There's a lot of good in the human race, but we aren't ready yet."

"I think you're crazy," said Kingsley, bitterly.

"Can't you see," asked Caroline, "what the human race right now would do to this city?"

"But magnetic power," wailed Kingsley, "and all those other things. Think of how they would help us. We need power and tools and all the knowledge we can get."

"You may take certain information with you," said the Engineer. "Whatever you think is wise. We will watch you and talk with you throughout the years, and it may be there will be times that you will wish our help."

Gary rose from the table. His hand fell on the Engineer's broad metal shoulder.

"And in the meantime there is work for you," he said. "A city to rebuild. The development of power stations to use the fifth-dimensional energy. Learning how to control and use that energy. Using it to control the universe. The day will come, unless we do something about it, that our universe will run down, will die the heat death. But with the eternal power of the inter-space, we can shape and control the universe, hold it to our needs."

It seemed that the metal man drew himself even more erect.

"It will be done," he said.

"We must work, not for Man alone, but for the entire universe," said Gary.

"That is right," said the Engineer.

Kingsley heaved himself to his feet.

"We should be leaving for Pluto," he said. "Our work here is done."

He stepped up to the Engineer. "Before we go," he said, "I would like to shake your hand."

"I do not understand," said the Engineer.

"It is a mark of respect," Caroline explained. "Assurance that we are friends. A sort of way to seal a pact."

"That is fine," said the Engineer. He thrust out his hand.

And then his thoughts broke. For the first time since they had met him, in this same room, there was emotion in his voice.

"We are so glad," he said. "We can talk to you and not feel so alone. Perhaps some day I can come and visit you."

"Be sure to do that," bellowed Herb. "I'll show you all the sights."

"Are you coming, Gary?" asked Caroline, but Gary didn't answer.

Some day Man would come home . . . home to this wondrous city of white stone, to marvel at its breathtaking height, at its vastness of design, at its far-flung symbol of achievement reared against an alien sky. Home to a planet where every power and every luxury and every achievement would be his. Home to a place that had grown out of a dream . . . the great dream of a greater people who had died, but in dying had passed along the heritage of their life to a new-spawned solar system. And more than that, had left another heritage in the hands and brains of good stewards who, in time, would give it up, in fulfillment of their charge.

But this city and this proud achievement were not for him, nor for Caroline, nor Kingsley, nor Herb, nor Tommy. Nor for the many generations that would come after them. Not so long as Man carried the old dead weight of primal savagery and hate, not so long as he was mean and vicious and petty, could he set foot here.

Before he reached this city, Man would travel long trails of bitter dust, would know the sheer triumphs of the starflung road. Galaxies would write new alphabets across the sky, and the print of many happenings would be etched upon the tape of time. New things would come and hold their sway and die. Great leaders would stand up and have their day and shuffle off into oblivion and silence. Creeds would rise and flourish and be sifting dust between the worlds. The night watch of stars would see great deeds, applaud great happenings, witness great defeat, weep over bitter sorrows.

"Just think," said Caroline. "We are going home."

"Yes," said Gary. "At last, we're going home."